OLD SCHOOL

OLD SCHOOL

a novel

Tobias Wolff

Alfred A. Knopf
New York
2004

THIS IS A BORZOI BOOK
PUBLISHED BY ALFRED A. KNOPF

www.aaknopf.com

Knopf, Borzoi Books, and the colophon are registered
trademarks of Random House, Inc.

Grateful acknowledgment is made to Henry Holt and
Company, LLC, for permission to reprint an excerpt from the
poem "Mending Wall" from *The Poetry of Robert Frost*, edited by
Edward Connery Lathem. Copyright © 1930, 1939, copyright ©
1969 by Henry Holt and Co., copyright © 1967 by Lesley Frost
Ballantine, copyright © 1958 by Robert Frost. Reprinted by
permission of Henry Holt and Company, LLC.

"Class Picture," "On Fire," and "Frost" previously appeared
in slightly different form in *The New Yorker*.

Library of Congress Cataloging-in-Publication Data
Wolff, Tobias, [date]
Old school : a novel / by Tobias Wolff.— 1st ed.
p.   cm.
ISBN 0-375-40146-6 (alk. paper)
1. Preparatory school students—Fiction.   2. Preparatory schools—
Fiction.   3. Creative writing—Fiction.   4. Teenage boys—Fiction.
5. New England—Fiction.   6. Authors—Fiction.   I. Title.
PS3573.O558O43 2003
813'.54—dc21
2003052930

Manufactured in the United States of America
Published November 9, 2003
Reprinted Five Times
Seventh Printing, February 2004

FOR MY TEACHERS

Why did you lie to me?
I always thought I told the truth.
Why did you lie to me?
Because the truth lies like nothing else and I love the truth.

Mark Strand, "Elegy for My Father"

I cannot begin to thank Catherine Wolff and Gary Fisketjon for the incalculable help they gave me in their many readings of this book; my particular thanks as well to Amanda Urban for her help, and for all her encouragement and support over the years.

CLASS PICTURE

Robert Frost made his visit in November of 1960, just a week after the general election. It tells you something about our school that the prospect of his arrival cooked up more interest than the contest between Nixon and Kennedy, which for most of us was no contest at all. Nixon was a straight arrow and a scold. If he'd been one of us we would have glued his shoes to the floor. Kennedy, though—here was a warrior, an ironist, terse and unhysterical. He had his clothes under control. His wife was a fox. And he read and wrote books, one of which, *Why England Slept*, was required reading in my honors history seminar. We recognized Kennedy; we could still see in him the boy who would have been a favorite here, roguish and literate, with that almost formal insouciance that both enacted and discounted the fact of his class.

But we wouldn't have admitted that class played any part in our liking for Kennedy. Ours was not a snobbish school, or so it believed, and we made this as true as we could. Everyone did chores. Scholarship students could declare themselves or not, as they wished; the school itself gave no sign. It was understood that some of the boys might get a leg up from their famous names or great wealth, but if privilege immediately gave them a place, the rest of us liked to think it was a perilous place. You could never advance in it, you could only try not to lose it by talking too much about the debutante parties you went to or the Jaguar you earned by turning sixteen. And meanwhile, absent other distinctions, you were steadily giving ground to a system of honors that valued nothing you hadn't done for yourself.

That was the idea, so deeply held it was never spoken; you breathed it in with the smell of floor wax and wool and boys living close together in overheated rooms. Never spoken, so never challenged. And the other part of the idea was that whatever you *did* do for yourself, the school would accept as proof of worth beyond any other consideration. The field was wide open. Like all schools, ours prized its jocks, and they gave good value, especially the wrestlers, who merrily wiped the mat with grim, grunting boys up and down the Eastern Seaboard. The school liked its wrestlers and football players but also its cutthroat debaters and brilliant scholars, its singers and chess champs, its cheerleaders and actors and musicians and wits, and, not least of all, its scribblers.

If the school had a snobbery it would confess to, this was its pride in being a literary place—quite aside from the glamorous writers who visited three times a year. The headmaster had studied with Robert Frost at Amherst and once published a collection of poetry, *Sonnets Against the Storm*, which it now pained him to be reminded of. Though listed in the library's card catalogue, the book had vanished and the headmaster was rumored to have destroyed it. Perhaps with reason; but how many other heads of school had published even one poem, good or bad, let alone a whole volume? Dean Makepeace had been a friend of Hemingway's during World War I and was said to have served as the model for Jake's fishing buddy Bill in *The Sun Also Rises*. The other English masters carried themselves as if they too were intimates of Hemingway, and also of Shakespeare and Hawthorne and Donne. These men seemed to us a kind of chivalric order. Even boys without bookish hopes aped their careless style of dress and the ritual swordplay of their speech. And at the headmaster's monthly teas I was struck by the way other masters floated at the fringe of their circle, as if warming themselves at a fire.

How did they command such deference—English teachers? Compared to the men who taught physics or biology, what did they really know of the world? It seemed to me, and not only to me, that they knew exactly what was most worth knowing. Unlike our math and science teachers, who modestly stuck to their subjects, they tended to be polymaths. Adept as they were at dissection, they would never leave a poem or a novel strewn about in pieces like some butchered frog reeking of formaldehyde. They'd stitch it back together with history and psychology, philosophy, religion, and even, on occasion, science. Without pandering to your presumed desire to identify with the hero of a story, they made you feel that what mattered to the writer had consequence for you, too.

Say you've just read Faulkner's "Barn Burning." Like the son in the story, you've sensed the faults in your father's character. Thinking about them makes you uncomfortable; left alone, you'd probably close the book and move on to other thoughts. But instead you are taken in hand by a tall, brooding man with a distinguished limp who involves you and a roomful of other boys in the consideration of what it means to be a son. The loyalty that is your duty and your worth and your problem. The goodness of loyalty and its difficulties and snares, how loyalty might also become betrayal—of the self and the world outside the circle of blood.

You've never had this conversation before, not with anyone.

And even as it's happening you understand that just as your father's troubles with the world—emotional frailty, self-doubt, incomplete honesty—will not lead him to set it on fire, your own loyalty will never be the stuff of tragedy. You will not turn bravely and painfully from your father as the boy in the story does, but forsake him without regret. And as you accept that separation, it seems to happen; your father's sad, fleshy face grows vague, and you blink it away and look up to where your master leans against his desk, one hand in a coat pocket, the other rubbing his bum knee as he listens desolately to the clever bore behind you saying something about bird imagery.

There was a tradition at my school by which one boy was granted a private audience with each visiting writer. We contended for this honor by submitting a piece of our own work, poetry if the guest was a poet, fiction if a novelist. The writer chose the winner a week or so before arriving. The winner had his poem or story published in the school newspaper, and, later, a photograph of him walking the headmaster's garden with the visiting writer.

By custom, only sixth formers, boys in their final year, were allowed to compete. That meant I had spent the last three years looking on helplessly as boy after boy was plucked from the crowd of suitors and invited to stroll between the headmaster's prize roses in the blessed and blessing presence of literature itself, to speak of deep matters and receive counsel, and afterward be able to say, You liked *By Love Possessed?* You're kidding. I mean, Jesus, you ought to hear Mary McCarthy on the subject of Cozzens . . .

It was hard to bear, especially when the winning manuscript came from the hand of someone you didn't like, or, worse, from a boy who wasn't even known to be a contender—though this had happened just once in my years of waiting in the wings, when an apparent Philistine named Hurst won an audience with Edmund Wilson for a series of satirical odes in Latin. But all the other winners came, predictably enough, from the same stockpond: boys who aced their English classes and submitted work to the school lit mag and hung around with other book-drunk boys.

The writers didn't know us, so no one could accuse them of playing favorites, but that didn't stop us from disputing their choices. How could Robert Penn Warren prefer Kit Morton's plain dying-grandmother story to Lance Leavitt's stream-of-consciousness monologue from the viewpoint of a condemned man smoking his last cigarette while pouring daringly profane contempt over the judgment of a world that punishes you for one measly murder while ignoring the murder of millions? It didn't seem right that Lance, who defied the decorums of language and bourgeois morality, should have to look on while Robert Penn Warren walked the garden with a sentimentalist like Kit (whose story, through its vulgar nakedness of feeling, had moved me to secret tears).

I'm not exaggerating the importance to us of these trophy meetings. We cared. And I cared as much as anyone, because I not only read writers, I read *about* writers. I knew that Maupassant, whose stories I loved, had been taken up when young by Flaubert and Turgenev; Faulkner by Sherwood Anderson; Hemingway by Fitzgerald and Pound and Gertrude Stein. All these writers were welcomed by other writers. It seemed to follow that you needed such a welcome, yet before this could happen you somehow, anyhow, had to *meet* the writer who was to welcome you. My idea of how this worked wasn't low or even practical. I never thought about making connections. My aspirations were mystical. I wanted to receive the laying on of hands that had written living stories and poems, hands that had touched the hands of other writers. I wanted to be anointed.

———

Frost's visit was announced in early October. At first the news made me giddy, but that night I grew morose with the dread of defeat. I couldn't sleep. Finally I got up and sat at my desk with two notebooks full of poetry I'd written when taking a break from stories. While my roommate muttered in his dreams I bent over the pages and read piece after piece like:

song (#8)

to the hopeless of the hopeless of the night
i sing my song and hopeless end my song
and do not pity me for i am without hope and
do not pity them for they are without hope and

There the poem ended. Beneath it I had written *fragment*. I'd written *fragment* beneath most of the poems in the notebooks, and this description was in every case accurate. Each of them had been composed in some fever of ardor or philosophy that deserted me before I could bring it to the point of significance. The few poems that I had finished seemed, in the hard circle of light thrown by the gooseneck lamp, even more disappointing. The beauty of a fragment is that it still supports the hope of brilliant completeness. I thought of stitching several of them together into a sequence, à la "The Waste Land," but that they would thereby become meaningful seemed too much to hope for.

I would have to write something new. The deadline for submission was three weeks away. I could write a poem in that time, but what kind of poem should I write? Aside from being good, it would have to stand out from those of my competitors. But at least I knew—barring some dark horse like Hurst—who my competitors were.

There were three.

George Kellogg was the editor of our literary review, *Trouba-dour*. The review was very old and still appeared in its original format, on stiff heavy pages, in an engraved typeface that made every poem and story look like a time-worn classic. I had wanted the editorship myself and lost it by a single vote of the outgoing board, which left me with a dreary consolation title: director of publication. This was a disappointment, but not a blow. George had earned the position, tirelessly soliciting manuscripts from other boys, burning the midnight oil to put the latest number to bed before deadline. I did none of those things. *Troubadour* was the only gallery I had for my work; it never occurred to me to recruit rivals.

The very fact that George had earned the editorship made it appear less enviable. I wasn't after an A in Citizenship. Not that George couldn't write. He was a well-schooled, proficient writer, mainly of poetry. He always wrote in traditional forms, the vil-lanelle in particular, and his subject was loneliness: an old man picking his way across a fairground the morning after the fair; a child waiting outside a Greyhound station for a ride that doesn't come; a darkened theater after everyone has left save one old woman slowly gathering her things, dreading the long walk home to her empty room.

She dons her scarf, she dons her balding fur;
She takes her time, 'til Time at last takes her.

You could tell, reading George's poetry, that he knew his stuff. His lines scanned, he used alliteration and personification. Metonymy. His poems always had a *theme* and were full of sym-pathy for the little people of the world. They bored me stiff but George had expertise and gave occasional intimations of power in reserve.

I didn't really believe he would win. He seemed more professor than writer, with his watch chain and hairy tweed cap and slow, well-considered speech. The effect was less stuffy than dear, and that was George's problem; he was too dear, too kind. I never heard him say a hard word about anyone, and it visibly grieved him when the rest of us made sport of our schoolmates, especially those with hopes of being published in *Troubadour*. At our editorial meetings he argued for almost every submission, even knowing that we could take only a fraction of them. It was maddening. You couldn't tell whether he actually liked a piece or just hated turning people down. This provoked the rest of us to an even greater ferocity of judgment than we were naturally inclined to.

George's benevolence did not serve his writing well. For all its fluent sympathy, it was toothless. I had some magazine pictures of Ernest Hemingway tacked above my desk. In one he was baring his choppers at the camera in a way that left no doubt of his capacity for rending and tearing, which seemed plainly connected to his strength as a writer.

Still, I knew better than to write George off. If he just once let a strong feeling get the better of his manners, he might land a good one. He could win.

So could Bill White, my roommate. Bill had already written most of a novel, the first chapter of which we'd published in *Troubadour*. Two men and a woman are isolated in a hunting lodge during a blizzard. The narrator does not explain who they are, how they got there, or why they're together. But as you read on, you begin to get the picture: one of the men is a famous actor, the woman is his wife, and the second man is a surgeon. The men are old friends, but it emerges that the actor's wife is having an affair with the surgeon, who, it turns out, had once saved the actor's life with an impromptu tracheotomy during a safari.

Have to take my hat off to you, said Montague. Tricky bit of tradecraft, given the circumstances. Storm blowing the damned tent down, and the beaters into the liquor. I shan't forget it.

Not at all, not at all, said Dr. Coates. The merest intern could have done as well—probably better.

I shan't forget it, Montague repeated. I'm forever in your debt, he added coldly.

Aren't we all, said Ashley, pouring herself another scotch. She stared at the falling snow. Whatever would we do without the good doctor's services?

You bitch, said Montague. You perfectly beautiful bitch.

Though Bill hadn't let me read the rest of his novel—he was letting it settle before the final polish—I doubted that the hunting party's meticulously described rifles would stay locked in their cases for long.

Bill's people weren't only genteel, they were gentile. So, I assumed, was Bill. He had bright green eyes and pale skin that flushed easily in heat or cold. His manner was courtly, amused, and for some reason he seemed especially amused by me, which I liked and also didn't like. He played varsity squash. It had never occurred to me that he might be Jewish until his father came to visit, the spring of the previous year. Mr. White was a widower and lived in Peru, where he owned a textile company. He had Bill invite me for dinner at the village inn, and seeing the two together produced a certain shock: both of them tall and fair and green-eyed, Mr. White an older version of his son in every respect save the Brooklyn in his voice and an almost eager warmth. He referred often to their family, and it soon became obvious that they were Jewish. I had roomed with Bill for two years by then and he'd never given me the slightest hint. Though I practiced some serious dissembling of my own, I'd never suspected it of Bill.

I thought of him as honest, if aloof. Who was he, really? All that time together, and it turned out I didn't know him any better than he knew me.

Mr. White gave us a good feed that night. He was a friendly, comfortable man, but I was still trying to catch up and I'm sure I looked at him with more than polite curiosity. If Bill noticed, he didn't let on and afterward gave no sign of feeling compromised by my knowledge that he was not who he seemed to be. That made me wonder if maybe he'd never meant to seem not Jewish—if my surprise was simply the effect of my own narrowness and anxiety.

I didn't really believe that, of course. I believed that Bill had meant to deceive, and that his aplomb in the face of discovery was not innocence but a further artifice by which he masked his disquiet and, intentionally or not, forced me to probe my own response. Why not? That's how I would've carried it off. We never talked about any of this, naturally. For a while I worried that Bill might hold what I knew against me, but he didn't seem to. Maybe he was relieved to have someone know. That I could understand, very well.

When the time came to choose roommates for our final year we didn't even bother to discuss it. Of course we would room together. Nobody got along better, even if real friendship eluded us.

Bill was a contender. His characters were stilted but he had confidence and his stories were eventful and closely detailed. Most of the work in *Troubadour* suffered from generality. The more general, the more universal—that seemed to be the guiding principle. Bill's talent was particularity. How the snow creaked underfoot on a very cold clear day, or what the low white sun looked like through a tangle of black branches. The tackiness of a just-oiled rifle stock, the tearing sound of a bored woman brushing out her long hair in front of a fire. Everything in his work was particular and true except the people. That hurt the longer pieces, but in Bill's shortest, most implicit stories, and in his occasional poems, the exactitude and poise of his writing could carry you away. He had me worried.

So did Jeff Purcell, known as Little Jeff because we had another Jeff Purcell in our class, his cousin—Big Jeff. In fact Little Jeff wasn't little and Big Jeff wasn't big, just bigger than Little Jeff, who resented Big Jeff, partly no doubt for inadvertently imposing this odious nickname on him. Little Jeff was a friend of mine, so like his other friends I called him Purcell.

Purcell habitually kept his arms folded across his chest like a Civil War general in a daguerrotype. This bellicose pose suited him. Under his bristling crew cut he cultivated a sulfurous gift for invective and contempt. He was the Herod of our editorial sessions, poised to strike down every innocent who presumed to offer us a manuscript. He had exacting standards: moral, political, aesthetic. Purcell even flouted the timeless protocol of pretending to admire the work of his fellow editors. At one of our meetings he declared that a story of mine called "Suicide Note" read as if it'd been written *after* the narrator blew his brains out.

Purcell came from a rich, social family, but you wouldn't have guessed it from his stories and poems; or maybe you would. His subject was the injustice of relations between high and low. He had written a ballad about a miner being sent deep into the earth to perish in a cave-in while the mine owner hand-feeds filet mignon to his hunting dogs, cooing to them in baby talk; and his last *Troubadour* piece was an epistolary story in which a general writes congratulatory letters to various grieving women after getting their husbands and sons slaughtered.

You may rejoice for your fallen hero, knowing that his heart was perforated for our glorious cause, and you and your little ones can rest assured that his missing head, wherever it may be, is filled with the

pride of sacrifice and radiant memories of the homeland for which he
died so eagerly.

This story was, I felt sure, inspired by a certain passage in A *Farewell to Arms*, but when it came up for consideration I bit my tongue and let it go. It wasn't bad. Cartoonish, of course, like all of Purcell's work, lurid and overwrought, to be sure, but venomously alive. Anyway, I myself was in debt to Hemingway—up to my ears. So was Bill. We even talked like Hemingway characters, though in travesty, as if to deny our discipleship: That is your bed, and it is a good bed, and you must make it and you must make it well. Or: Today is the day of meatloaf. The meatloaf is swell. It is swell but when it is gone the not-having meatloaf will be tragic and the meatloaf man will not come anymore.

All of us owed someone, Hemingway or cummings or Kerouac—or all of them, and more. We wouldn't have admitted to it but the knowledge was surely there, because imitation was the only charge we never brought against the submissions we mocked so cruelly. There was no profit in it. Once crystallized, consciousness of influence would have doomed the collective and necessary fantasy that our work was purely our own. Even Purcell kept mum on that subject.

He was a threat. His attack was broad, even crude, but you could feel his discomfort with the cushion he'd been born on, and his fear that it would turn him into one of the fatuous bloodsuckers he wrote about. If he humanized his targets, muted his voice, used a knife instead of a cudgel . . . Yet he didn't necessarily have to do any of that. In a field of stiffs, one of his cartoons could win for simply being alive.

———

These, then, were the boys who stood between me and Robert Frost. Of course there were other self-confessed writers in my form, but I'd read their English papers and *Troubadour* submissions and seen nothing to worry me except their desire. So much desire! Why did so many of us want to be writers? It seemed unreasonable. But there were reasons.

The atmosphere of our school crackled with sexual static. We had the occasional dance with Miss Cobb's Academy and a few other girls' schools, but these brief affairs only cranked up the charge; and though from day to day we saw the master's wives, Roberta Ramsey alone had the goods to enter our dreams. The absence of an actual girl to compete for meant that every other prize became feminized. For honors in sport, scholarship, music, and writing we cracked our heads together like mountain rams, and to make your mark as a writer was equal as proof of puissance to a brilliant season on the gridiron.

This aspect of my ambition was obscure to me at the time. But there was another that I did recognize, though vaguely, and almost in spite of myself: the problem of class.

Our school was proud of its hierarchy of character and deeds. It believed that this system was superior to the one at work outside, and that it would wean us from habits of undue pride and deference. It was a good dream and we tried to live it out, even while knowing that we were actors in a play, and that outside the theater was a world we would have to reckon with when the curtain closed and the doors were flung open.

Class was a fact. Not just the clothes a boy wore, but how he wore them. How he spent his summers. The sports he knew how to play. His way of turning cold at the mention of money, or at the spectacle of ambition too nakedly revealed. You felt it as a depth of ease in certain boys, their innate, affable assurance that they would not have to struggle for a place in the world, that it had already been reserved for them; a depth of ease or, in the case of Purcell and a few others, a sullen antipathy toward the padding that hemmed them in and muffled the edges of life. Yet even in the act of kicking against it they were defined by it, and protected by it, and to some extent unconscious of it. Purcell himself had a collection of first editions you'd almost have to own a mine to pay for.

These things I understood instinctively. I never gave them voice, not even within the privacy of my thoughts, precisely because the school's self-conception was itself unspoken and thus inarguable. From my first days there I grasped and gratefully entered the dream but at the same time behaved as if I knew better, as in the following instance.

The summer before entering the school I'd worked as a dishwasher in the kitchen crew at a YMCA camp outside Seattle. I was the youngest, and the other guys rode me pretty hard until Hartmut, the chef, saw what was going on and headed them off. He did this obliquely, never defending me directly but bearing down on the hardest kidders by giving them the shit work, the grease trap or the fryolator. Eventually some subliminal sense of cause and effect must have taken hold, because they eased up and then we all got along fine. After dinner, when the kitchen was polished to his satisfaction, Hartmut let us play Tom Lehrer albums on his old portable. Though he didn't get the jokes, he enjoyed our hilarity. Ah! You boys! You crazy crazy boys!

Hartmut was from Austria. He'd been in the States for many years but his English was eccentric and often ludicrous. He wore an actual chef's hat and a white uniform that he changed every day. He cooked for those hot-dog-loving kids as if they were royalty—soufflés, pastries of airy lightness, quiches, many-layered tortes. He had great pride and didn't allow himself to notice when the little pagans made gagging noises over their eggs Benedict.

Pink and thick and strong, Hartmut ran his kitchen like a ship, everything in its place, all orders to be obeyed on the instant. Though he appeared not to have a family, his love for children was obvious and utterly benevolent. He also loved music. When the record player wasn't blasting out waltzes and light opera, he whistled and sang. Some of his melodies were catchy and stuck in my head. And that's what landed me in trouble.

I'd been at the school for five or six weeks, no more. I was struggling in my classes but every morning I felt a rush of joy to wake to the bells ringing in the clock tower and go to my window and think, My God! I'm really here! In my pleasure I was whistling a tune of Hartmut's as I climbed the dormitory stairs after breakfast. Gershon, one of the school handymen, was a few steps ahead of me, carrying a laundry bag on his narrow shoulders. He had a plodding gait even on the level; here on the stairs he barely moved at all. I was afraid I'd bump into him if I tried to pass, so I kept pace a few steps behind, whistling all the while. Gershon gave off a stale smell that I'd whiffed before but never so strongly as in this tight passage.

He slowed even more. I hung back obligingly and continued to whistle, my song resounding pleasantly in the stone stairwell. Then Gershon stopped and turned his long gray face, the laundry bag slumped on his shoulders like a lamb in a Bible illustration. I could hear him breathe, fast and shallow. He said something in what I thought was another language—I knew he was a foreigner of some kind. His too-white teeth clicked as he talked; I watched them with helpless fascination. Then he stopped. He appeared to be waiting for an answer.

Name! he said. Vat your name!

I told him.

Go den! Go! Go!

I nudged past him and went to my room, and by the time

classes started I'd written it off as a misunderstanding: the old crab must've thought I'd been trying to hurry him. When a prefect called me out of Latin during second period and sent me to the dean's office, I assumed it was to receive a lecture about my abysmal grades. I was on scholarship, and had been nervously fearing a summons.

I hadn't met Dean Makepeace yet but I knew who he was: he was Ernest Hemingway's friend. He closed the door behind me and looked me over without a word of greeting, then motioned me toward the hot seat. He let himself down in the chair behind the desk and began to leaf through a file. Mine, I supposed.

He reeked of tobacco. Most of the masters did. It usually seemed a pleasant, paternal smell, though in my worried state I was nearly sickened by it. Before now I had seen Dean Makepeace only from a distance, at his table in the dining hall or tapping his way across campus, often conducted by an escort of older boys. With his height and his nose and his long black cane he'd appeared regal but benign. At this range he seemed neither. Dense white hairs bristled from his ears and nostrils. Cigarette smoke had tinged his white moustache with yellow, and his suit jacket was smudged with ash. I had the impression that he wasn't actually reading the file, just occupying himself with it while he decided how to carve me up, or maybe to give me time to feel the full weight of my laziness and ingratitude and the complete disappointment of everyone with hopes for me.

My chair had a high ladder-back that held me bolt upright. Shelves of dark, uniformly bound books rose up on either side, floor to high ceiling. Much as I loved books, there was something unfriendly about these; when I came across Meredith's poem "Lucifer in Starlight" later that year and read the line *The army of unalterable law,* I thought not of the stars but of those looming tomes. Behind his desk the leaded window was open to the breeze. I heard a burst of laughter from one of the classrooms on the quad. It stopped suddenly.

Dean Makepeace laid the file on the desk. Explain yourself, he said.

Well, sir, I was pretty far behind when I got here.

What?

Not to make excuses. I know I need to work harder.

Don't change the subject. Do you have any idea what that man has been through?

Sir?

You heard me. I am unable to understand how anyone could behave like this to a man in Gershon's position. Please explain.

Dean Makepeace said all this calmly enough, but I wilted under his gaze. He wasn't angry. Anger, which I knew to be transient and generally at least part theater, I was used to and could easily bear. What I saw was dislike, which can't be shrugged off, which abides.

I didn't mean to hurry Gershon, I said. I'm sorry if he got that impression.

Oh, was *that* it? He wasn't moving fast enough, so you thought you'd give him a little marching music. Why don't you strike up the band for me?

Sir?

I want you to sing me what you sang to Gershon.

Well, I was whistling a song. I don't know the words.

Whistle away, then.

My mouth was so dry I couldn't get a note out. I made a few false starts and gave up.

Come on. Let's have it.

I can't.

You were doing okay this morning, weren't you? All right— hum the damned thing.

I did. It sounded different, hummed, but I could tell Dean Makepeace recognized it and that this wasn't helping matters. I stopped and said, Sir, what is this song?

Don't play dumb with me, boy.

I'm not! I'm not playing dumb. What did I do wrong? The self-pity of this question brought me close to tears.

You say you don't know what this song is?

I shook my head furiously.

Where did you learn it, then?

A man I worked with. Hartmut. I picked it up from him. The tune.

You must know other songs.

Yes sir.

Many other songs. Yet of all the songs you know, you just happened to whistle this one to Gershon. To *Gershon*, of all people!

I wasn't whistling *to* him. I was just whistling. And Gershon was there.

Was there some occasion for this outbreak of melody?

Nothing special. I was feeling happy, that's all.

Dean Makepeace leaned back in his chair. Happy. What were you happy about?

Being here.

He stroked his moustache. You'll want to be somewhat discreet about that, he said. Honestly, boy, what have you heard about Gershon?

Nothing. I see him around, that's all.

So you don't know anything about him?

No sir.

Have you ever heard of the "Horst Wessel Song"?

You mean the Christmas carol?

No, no. The "Horst Wessel Song" is a Nazi marching song, and a very ugly piece of work it is, too. That's what you were singing. Whistling.

Then it all came home. As a child of the superior, disgusted, victorious nation I had the usual store of images to go with the words Nazi and Jew, and I was putting Gershon's face to them even before Dean Makepeace began to tell me what had befallen Gershon and his family, of whom none had survived but a daughter who was now in a French mental hospital. As he spoke I felt my eyes tearing up, partly from pity and also because the sadness of the story gave me cover to mourn my own plight, unjustly accused and humiliated by a great man of the school only a few weeks into my first term—a man I'd hoped to study with one day, who might even befriend me.

It was too much. I started to weep—to blubber. My lack of control mortified me and I turned in my chair, hunched away from him. I tried to stop but couldn't. I felt a hand on my back. Dean Makepeace kept it there for a moment, then gave my shoulder a squeeze and left the room.

By the time he came back I had exhausted myself. He offered me a glass of water and waited beside my chair. The water was cold. I drank most of it in a gulp, then finished it off and handed Dean Makepeace the glass. Though he didn't say anything, I understood that our meeting was over. I got up and told him I was sorry about Gershon, that I'd had no idea . . .

I know. I know you didn't.

But *how* did he know? How could he, in the face of such an inconceivable coincidence? Surely some doubt remained. I had the means to prove myself, but already knew I'd never make use of it.

Dean Makepeace walked me to the door. He shook my hand and said, If you'll be good enough to clear things up with Gershon, we can put this to rest. The sooner the better. Tonight, say. After dinner.

And get those grades up.

———

CLASS PICTURE

Gershon lived in the basement of Holmes, the sixth-form dormitory, just off the boiler room. Even down there I could hear the boys upstairs, blustering and braying, full of the knowledge that at last the school was theirs. Gershon let me inside the door but no farther, and waited while I began to explain myself.

The room was close and smelled of onions. Gershon had been sewing something, and the table was strewn with scraps of cloth. No books in sight. No pictures. Insulated pipes ran across the ceiling.

As I talked he kept his face averted, his mouth set in a puckered line; he wasn't wearing his teeth. He would neither speak to me nor give any sign that he was listening. It was obvious that he regarded my visit as a galling evolution of the ugliness I'd already dealt him, and that he'd agreed to it only because he thought he had no choice. I tried to keep my explanation simple and slow. I couldn't be sure he understood me, though I had the feeling he did and that he didn't believe a word I was saying.

The story sounded incredible even to me, and its grotesque, improbable accidents—that song, of all songs; Gershon, of all people—robbed my voice of conviction and, finally, of sense. I started to tell him about learning the song from Hartmut, then got lost in describing what a nice guy Hartmut was and how he must not have known what the song was about, or maybe he'd forgotten and just remembered the tune . . . Gershon stared into the corner, sucking his cheeks, enduring me, waiting for the lies to stop and for me to leave him in peace. And still I pushed on. I wanted him to believe me, for my own sake of course, but also for his, so he'd know there weren't any Nazis here.

Again it occurred to me that I could prove my case: I could tell him that my own father was Jewish. This was true, though he himself never mentioned the fact, not even to me, his only child. My mother had told me only a year before, not long before she died, and I had no idea what it should mean to me. I had been raised Catholic; up to now my teachers had been nuns and the occasional priest, my social world entirely gentile. I knew nothing about Jews except some of their recent history. If I'd learned that my father was descended from Southern Baptists, would that make me a Southern Baptist? No. I would still be the boy I'd been the day before I came into this knowledge. The same with his Jewish ancestry. It was a fact but not a defining fact, neither to be asserted nor denied.

But it had come to a kind of question twice that day, and both times I'd chosen to deny it. Telling Dean Makepeace or Gershon about my father might not have cleared me; Jews can be savage Jew-baiters, as everyone knows, but I didn't know. I thought I held a trump card, and my refusal to play it amounted to a deception.

The scene with Gershon could be spun into a certain kind of story. The new boy comes to clear things up with the cranky handyman he's unwittingly affronted and ends up confiding his own Jewish blood, whereupon the handyman melts and a friendship ensues. In time the man who has lost his sons becomes a true father to the boy, enfolding him in the tradition his own false father has denied him. And what irony: the ambitious, upward-striving boy must descend to a basement room to learn the wisdom not being taught in the snob factory upstairs.

Fat chance. I wanted out of there, and I was confiding nothing. I'd let Gershon think the worst of me before I would claim any connection to him, or implicate myself in the fate that had beached him in this room. Why would I want to talk my way into his unlucky tribe? All this came over me as a gathering sense of suffocation. I stammered out a final apology and left, taking the stairs at a run as soon as the door clicked shut behind me.

It had been different that morning with Dean Makepeace,

calmer and clearer. I simply decided that it would be better not to use the Jewish defense. There was no obvious reason for being cagey. In my short time at the school I'd seen no bullying or manifest contempt of that kind, and never did. Yet it seemed to me that the Jewish boys, even the popular ones, even the athletes, had a subtly charged field around them, an air of apartness. And somehow the feeling must have settled in me that this apartness did not emanate from the boys themselves, from any quality or wish of their own, but from the school—as if some guardian spirit, indifferent to their personal worth, had risen from the fields and walkways and weathered stone to breathe that apartness upon them.

This was no more than a tremor of apprehension, and though I acted on it I did not allow it to occupy my thoughts. But it never really deserted me. It became a shadow on my faith in the school. Much as I wanted to believe in its egalitarian vision of itself, I never dared put it to the test.

Other boys must have felt the same intimations. Maybe that was why so many of them wanted to become writers. Maybe it seemed to them, as it did to me, that to be a writer was to escape the problems of blood and class. Writers formed a society of their own outside the common hierarchy. This gave them a power not conferred by privilege—the power to create images of the system they stood apart from, and thereby to judge it.

I hadn't heard anyone speak of a writer as having power. Truth, yes. Wit, understanding, even courage—but never power. We had talked in class about Pasternak and his troubles, and the long history of Russian writers being imprisoned and killed for not writing as the Party wished. Augustus Caesar had sent our Latin master's beloved Ovid into exile. And when the progressive Mr. Ramsey—himself a gift from England—wanted to show us what mushrooms we all were, he recalled our nation's inhospitality to *Lolita*, which he considered the century's greatest novel since *Ulysses*—another victim of churlish American censors!

Yet the effect of all these stories was to make me feel not Caesar's power, but his fear of Ovid. And why would Caesar fear Ovid, except for knowing that neither his divinity nor all his legions could protect him from a good line of poetry.

ON FIRE

The day before our Frost poems were due we had a fire at the school. Fire was the great nightmare. Early in the century a residential house had burned to the ground with thirteen boys inside, and the shock of those deaths could still be felt in my day. They were known as the Blaine Boys, after the house they lived in. Their group photo, taken for the yearbook they never saw, hung in Blaine Memorial Hall, where we sixth formers gathered for talk and singing after dinner. I was drawn to the picture. I studied their serious faces (no clowning for the camera in those days), their way of sprawling against one another, leaning back to back, one boy resting his head on another's shoulder. The sense of loss I felt wasn't just for their lives: how artlessly tender, how easy they were together.

Their housemaster had been drinking in the village when it happened. He left for another boys' school the next year and then, the story went, drifted to another, and another, never to find rest.

The fire was said to have been started by a cigarette. How anyone could know that, we didn't ask. It was revealed truth. And it led to a commandment: Thou shalt not smoke. Get caught and you were out; no discussion, no exceptions. Even the softest masters were without mercy on this point. Two or three smokers a year got the boot, given just enough time to pack and call their parents. A boy would return from swimming practice and find his roommate gone, hangers tinkling in an empty closet, the other mattress stripped and doubled over. No announcements were made and no lessons preached. This swift and silent erasure of smokers from the school served grim notice on the rest of us. It was the same fate suffered by thieves and violators of the Honor Code, and smoking was meant to be seen in that light, as a betrayal of us all.

So we had fair warning and plenty of it—in spite of which an unteachable cadre of resolutes, including me, kept smoking anyway. I'd sneaked the occasional gasper since eighth grade but at school it became an obsession. Crazy as I was for cigarettes, my true addiction was to the desperate, all-or-nothing struggle to maintain a habit in the face of unceasing official vigilance. Always on the scout for new venues, I smoked in freezers and storage lockers and steam tunnels. I joined the Classical Music Club so I could smoke in the bathrooms of the concert halls we visited, and went out for cross-country so I could smoke while running in the woods. I kept a store of spearmint Life Savers to mask my breath and used a holder so my fingers wouldn't stain. It was fretful, laborious work, but when I took that first deep drag I went dizzy with pleasure, not least the pleasure of getting away with it one more time.

Then I almost got caught. I'd been smoking in the basement of the chapel with a boy who was discovered there by the chaplain just minutes after I left. I was putting music in the choir stalls—my chore that week, and my excuse for being there— when the two of them came upstairs and walked down the aisle, the chaplain sad but decided, holding the boy by the elbow, and the boy . . . I could only glance at him and then I looked away, but I saw enough. For the rest of the afternoon my gut clenched at the approach of any master. I was afraid the other boy had given me away, not to save himself—no chance of that—but in a fit of clear-cutting confession, or resentment at my escape. He didn't, though. He went out the gates alone.

I had seen his face. I knew what was happening to him. He was in free fall, and still trying to believe he was only in a dream of falling. He lived in New York. It would be a long night's ride for him, on the train, by himself. I could easily see myself on that train. My journey wouldn't stop in New York, though. I'd have to catch the gritty Century to Chicago, then change to the Great Northern—day after day of rolling past factories and fields and deserts and mountains but seeing none of it, gazing at my own stunned reflection in the glass as every click of the wheels took me farther from school. Lying sleepless in bed that night, I saw my school as if from an impossible distance, heading across the plains in a darkened railway car, back to the melancholy and muddle of life with my father. I pictured the black-beamed dining hall loud with voices. The chapel windows blazing red on winter afternoons. The comradely sound of the glee club practicing, the scrape of skates on the outdoor rink, a certain chair in the library, the deep peace of the library, the faces of my friends. I saw the school as if I'd left it forever, and the thought made me sick at heart. I got up and collected my suicide kit of cigarettes and lighter and holder from their hiding places and went to the bathroom at the end of the hall and stuffed it all into the trash can. I never smoked at school again.

But the temptation was persistent, and sometimes I could almost hear the old crew puffing away in the basements and attics. So my first thought when the sirens came wailing up the drive that Sunday afternoon was that one of those poor fiends had started a fire somewhere, and would pay the price that very hour. Who would it be?

I was coming out of the library. From the top of the steps I could see a thick braid of smoke twisting up over the old field house. Thrill-starved boys poured out of the dorms and halls, with a few masters trying to form them into groups or at least slow them down, all to no effect. I followed, my notebook under my arm.

I had been holed up most of the weekend, trying to finish my poem for the competition. What I'd been working on was a hunter's elegiac meditation over the body of an elk he's killed after tracking it for days through the mountains. This wasn't typical of my poems, abstract and void of narrative as they tended to be. It fell into the pattern of a group of my stories in which a young fellow named Sam evaded the civilizing demands of his socialite mother and logger-baron father by fleeing into the forests of the Pacific Northwest, where he did much hunting and fishing and laconic romancing with free-spirited women he met on the trail. I had begun this series innocently enough, in unconscious tribute to the Nick Adams stories, but over time it had evolved into something less honest. I wanted to be taken for Sam by my schoolmates, who knew nothing of my life back in Seattle.

But this poem was giving me a headache. For one thing, how was the hunter, having trailed the elk so far into the woods, going to get it out? How big was an elk, anyway? Really big, I guessed— so after offering thanks to the spirit of the elk for giving him all that meat, the hunter was going to look ridiculous walking away with one lousy haunch over his shoulder. Maybe I should've made it a regular deer. But *deer* didn't have the majesty of *elk*. There was a lot to fix, and the poem was due the next morning.

The day had turned cold. A storm had blown off the last of the leaves a few nights earlier, and the bare black trees made it seem even colder. I fell in with a younger boy, a fourth former whose recent submission to *Troubadour* we had not yet rejected, though we probably would. I kept waiting for him to ask about it, but as we approached the fire he got excited and ran ahead without a word on the subject.

The crowd had gathered around the old field house at the near end of the football field. The firemen stood by their truck drinking coffee and taking turns with the hose. No flames were visible, though I could hear the water seethe as it hit the roof. The shingles had burned through here and there, exposing a sheet of charred subroofing that sent up a greasy hiss of smoke as the firemen played the hose over it.

I asked the boy next to me how the fire had started, and without taking his eyes off the field house he mumbled something about Jeff Purcell.

Purcell. The news rattled me because this was my friend, and because he'd invited me to spend Thanksgiving vacation with his family in Boston, and now I could look forward to nothing better than another stretch with my boring grandfather and his boring wife in a housing development outside Baltimore.

False alarm! It wasn't my Purcell, Little Jeff, who'd started the fire, it was his cousin. Big Jeff was a vegetarian, the only one in our class, whose love of animals extended to an ugly black rat he somehow kept hidden in his room and carried around at night in a pocket of his dressing gown. Big Jeff would've been a figure of fun among us if not for his great friendliness and his trust in everyone else's goodwill. When you did tease him he didn't get it, he just looked at you like a puppy wondering why in God's name you'd tied a can to his tail. Big Jeff was devoted to Purcell. He haunted his room and patiently endured his abuse just to sit in the corner and watch him shave or do push-ups or dress for dinner, and listen to him pronounce his opinions and anathemas. He wasn't stupid, Big Jeff. He did well in his science classes, and what he cared about, he knew about. He'd made himself an authority on how animals were raised and slaughtered, and as we tucked into our roast beef he spared us no detail as to how it got from the pasture to the plate.

Big Jeff had another passion, and in pursuit of this he almost burned down the old field house. He believed that our destiny was to leave Earth behind and colonize other planets. In our fifth-form year he'd started the Rocket Club, and though he couldn't find any members in our class—we were too busy licking our chops for a great big bite of *this* planet—he did manage to recruit a few younger boys out of the Science Fiction Club. On Sunday afternoons the Rocket Club met at the football field under the eye of the chemistry master and shot off whatever they'd cooked up in the lab that week. Big Jeff had been experimenting with a two-stage rocket, but instead of going straight up his missile cut a few loops and crashed into the field house roof, where the explosive booster detonated in a clump of old pine needles and leaves. *Whoosh!*

I wish they'd kicked him out, Purcell told me that night.

I laughed. I thought he was joking.

We were walking back to our dorm after an editorial meeting. We left the brick path and cut across the grass, which was stiff with frost and rustled under our feet.

I know it sounds terrible, Purcell said, but I do. I wish they'd kicked him out.

Why would they do that? He didn't break any rules.

Did you see him at dinner tonight? He was doing everything but taking bows, like some kind of celebrity.

He *is* some kind of celebrity, actually.

Big Jeff. Big Jeff. When I was a baby they actually stuck him in the same crib with me. It's true. They say you can't remember that far back but I do. That hound-dog face staring at me, you think I could forget that? Kindergarten—the desk in front of mine. Always fidgeting, always looking for something, always with his hand up. I can still see the light shining through his ears. Grade school, camp, vacations—man, you don't know what it's like. Big Jeff and Little Jeff. Whatever college I end up at, he'll be there, waiting in my room. We'll probably get buried in the same coffin. Me and Big Jeff. Big Jeff and Little Jeff, *ad* fucking *aeternum*.

I started a new poem that night. It was the fire that got me going, that and the firemen in their open rubber coats and high gaping boots, the looks they sneaked at us and the masters and the school itself, pretending to let their glances skate over us but taking it all in. Their curiosity had made me look around too. For a moment I saw this place as I had first seen it: how beautiful it was, and how odd. I felt its seclusion and how we'd come to resemble each other in that seclusion. We dressed so much alike that the inflections we did allow ourselves—tasseled loafers for the playboy, a black turtleneck for the rebel—were probably invisible to an outsider. Our clothes, the way we wore our hair, the very set of our mouths, all this marked us like tribal tattoos.

The firemen looked us over, and we looked them over. Visitors snapped us to attention. There was one fireman in particular I found myself watching. He had tired-looking eyes, and held himself a little apart. He was less covert than the others in sizing us up. I thought about him after they finished and drove away.

That was how I came to write my new poem, a narrative in which I described a fireman the morning after a big blaze. He's been the hero that night, braving walls of flame to rescue a little girl. Now it's over. He goes home and it's Saturday morning and his son is watching TV. He fries himself some eggs but doesn't eat them. He's oppressed by the crumbs on the kitchen table, the dirty cereal bowls, the smell of burnt toast and last night's fish. The television is too loud. Then he's on his feet and in the living room and he's just yelled something, he doesn't know what, and his boy is looking at him with coldness and disdain.

I thought writing should give me pleasure, and generally it did. But I didn't enjoy writing this poem. I did it almost grudgingly, yet in a kind of heat too. Maybe it was good, maybe not. Maybe it wasn't even a poem, only a fragment of a story in broken lines. I couldn't tell. It was too close to home. It *was* home: my mother gone; my father, though no fireman, wounded by my disregard as I was appalled by his need; the mess, the noise, the smells, all of it just like our place on a Saturday morning; the sense of time dying drop by drop, of stalled purpose and the close, aquarium atmosphere of confinement and repetition. I could hear and see everything in that apartment, right down to the pattern in the Formica tabletop. I could see myself there, and didn't want to. Even more, I didn't want anyone else to.

I submitted the elk-hunter poem. "Red Snow," I called it.

FROST

The day after John F. Kennedy won the presidency, George Kellogg won the audience with Robert Frost. Our paper printed his poem in a box on the front page, a dramatic monologue in which an old farmer feels the bite of mortality on the first cold day of autumn. George had used an odd mixture of tones. At one moment the farmer is lyrically drooling over the sight of the hired girl milking a cow:

> Old rooster struts the rafters while the barncat begs
> Mewing at her feet in the stall where Flossie stands,
> As with swift hard strokes of her soft white hands
> She pulls the foaming cream into the pail between her legs.

Then a few stanzas down he's a terse fatalist:

> Corn's high in the silo, hay's stacked in the loft,
> Cordwood's halfway to the roof, doorcracks plugged with
>   clay.
> So let come what will, hard ground, short day,
> I've done all I am able—and after all, the snow is soft.

The poem was entitled, shamelessly, "First Frost."

In his telephone interview about the poem he'd chosen over all the others, Robert Frost told our reporter: *Young Kellogg has had some fun at this old man's expense, and I guess this old man can stand some fun, if it isn't too expensive.* He said he liked the joke of the milkmaid having soft hands. *All the milkmaids I ever had to do with could've gone bare-knuckle with Jim Corbett and made him bleed for his purse.* Frost suggested that a few winters on a farm wouldn't hurt any young poet, *to learn that snow is no metaphor, if nothing else. But I guess I've dipped my bucket there a time or two, and your fellow Kellogg has caught me fair and square.*

I was astonished that Frost could've read the poem as anything but an act of fawning servility. But no, he seemed to think that George had written some sort of burlesque, that he was using the poet's manner and material—perhaps his very *name*—to give him the needle. Frost sounded like a man who'd been stung by a taunt, showing he could take it and come back with some chaff of his own. Still, he'd paid George the ultimate compliment of choosing the poem. How hurt could he be?

I read the poem several times, and began to imagine that maybe it *was* satiric, and thus better than I'd first thought. But George set me straight when I went to his room that afternoon to congratulate him.

What did you think of the poem, he asked me.

I like it, way to go! George, you're going to meet Robert Frost!

Did you think I was . . . how did Mr. Frost put it—having fun at his expense?

Well, I guess you could read it that way.

You could?

It's possible.

Oh, jeez. He slumped like a puppet, taking no care to hide his distress. He still had his tie on, a knitted tie with a flat bottom. It looked crocheted; it looked like a doily. Our biology master wore ties like that but George was the only boy you'd catch dead in one. He was both the oldest and the youngest of us, the most fuddy-duddy and innocent, and I could see that his innocence extended to this question of sardonic intent. His poem, alas, was perfectly serious.

But you don't have to read it as parody, I said. You can also read it as tribute. You know, the farm, the folksy tone, the snow. It's like you're paying your respects to him—tipping your hat, so to speak.

Exactly! George sat across from me on his roommate's bed. That's exactly how I meant it, as an *homage*. He looked at me with such gratitude that I couldn't help throwing another log on the fire.

And of course the title, I said.

You like the title?

All those layers of meaning. "First Frost" as in, literally, the first frost of the year. Then there's the symbolic sense of here comes winter, i.e., death, but also *rest*, right? The snow is soft, *after all*, after all the hard work he's spent his whole life doing— soft and white like the girl's hands. *After all*, he's gonna get what he wants—unless I'm just reading this stuff into it.

No! No, it's all there.

Then, I said, the crowning touch. "First Frost" as in *first*, Frost—as in Frost is tops, Frost is the best, Frost is number one.

Exactly! Exactly. But it's not *just* an *homage*.

Of course not. You'd never find that business with the girl in one of his poems. Foaming cream. The pail between her legs. That doesn't sound like Frost. Doesn't really sound like you, either, to tell the truth.

It is something of a new direction for me. He looked down,

controlling a smile. I have to admit, the female character got away from me somewhat. Has that ever happened to you—someone you're writing about suddenly becomes real?

Now and then.

She became very real to me. This will sound strange, but I knew her. And I'm not talking about just metaphysically. It was physical too. In fact, when I was working on her part of the poem I found myself in a state of, you know . . . arousal. Has that ever happened to you?

Nope. I got up to leave. Look, you should probably keep that to yourself, George. You know how immature some of these guys can be.

Once a week the sixth-form Honors English Seminar was invited to eat dinner at the headmaster's table. He'd once been an English master himself and enjoyed our company, enough to be liable to the charge of favoritism; you'd never find him playing host to Honors Chemistry. He required literary conversation. If a couple of us talked up a book he hadn't read, he wrote down the title and read it himself, then put us through our paces. Dinner at his table often ran late, the headmaster forcing some booster to explain an enthusiasm he found baffling, while the rest of us, elbows planted in a waste of cups and napkins and half-eaten rolls, chimed in with our own judgments and dissents. The headmaster took the gloves off and let us do the same—a liberty we preserved by putting the gloves back on when we stood up to leave. I loved the passion, the self-forgetfulness of those nights, though more than once my swelling heart clenched at the sight of the dining-hall staff, all other tables stripped and set for breakfast, wearily waiting for us to shut up so they could finish their work and go home.

It was our headmaster who had persuaded Frost to visit. He

always called his old teacher Mr. Frost, and a few of us tried
that ourselves a time or two, until we saw the headmaster wince.
Then we all understood that Frost or Robert Frost was fine for us,
but that despite its apparently greater formality, Mr. Frost was
reserved for those who could claim acquaintance.

All of us understood, that is, but George Kellogg. Once
George sank his teeth into Mr. Frost he wasn't about to let go,
and seized any chance to say it. He was completely blind to the
headmaster's discomfort, his helpless hunch and shudder at every
repetition of the blunder. None of us had the heart to straighten
him out, and of course the headmaster couldn't do it without
sounding ridiculous: *I get to say Mr. Frost, but you don't!* It was a
nuance of etiquette as inexplicable as a joke, and George wasn't
snob enough to get it. But now, by a quirk of fate, he was going
to meet Robert Frost on his own, and afterward what had been
presumptuous would become impeccable—without George ever
knowing it!

Purcell fell in with me outside the dining hall and declared
his astonishment that George's poem had been selected. His
respect for Frost's intelligence, he said, had suffered irreversible
damage.

George's poem isn't that bad, I said, if you read it a certain
way.

As a take-off, you mean.

Right, as a take-off.

But it isn't a take-off.

It could be. That's how Frost read it.

But it isn't. And you know that.

It doesn't matter what I know.

Bullshit.

It doesn't. Let's say you find it in a bottle. You're walking on
the beach and you find George's poem in a bottle. You don't

know anything about the person who wrote it, you just have the poem. You'd probably read it as a take-off.

Frost. I don't know why I even bothered submitting anything, given how he writes. I mean, he's still using *rhyme*.

Yeah, so?

Rhyme is bullshit. Rhyme says that everything works out in the end. All harmony and order. When I see a rhyme in a poem, I know I'm being lied to. Go ahead, laugh! It's true—rhyme's a completely bankrupt device. It's just wishful thinking. Nostalgia.

I'm not laughing at you, I said, and I wasn't. What I was laughing at was the thought of George Kellogg getting aroused over his own poem. But Purcell was offended and turned away. Good thing, too. To prove I wasn't laughing at him I would've told him about George. He'd have told everyone else, and George would have gotten endless grief, and I would have despised myself.

If, as Talleyrand said, loyalty is a matter of dates, virtue itself is often a matter of seconds.

Robert Frost arrived during dinner. When he appeared in the dining hall, slowly crossing from the side door with the headmaster, gingerly mounting the two steps to the high table, the ordinary din died almost to silence. We kept eating and tried not to stare, but we couldn't help ourselves.

Frost let himself down into the chair at the headmaster's right, facing out over the room. He bent his big white head as he arranged his napkin, taking his time. He seemed deeply absorbed in the problem of the napkin. He looked up, nodded at something the headmaster said, and gravely surveyed the hall. The door to the kitchen swung open: a clatter of pans, someone shouting; the door swung to and the silence resumed. Then Dean Makepeace rose at the head of his table and turned toward Frost and began to clap, each report of his hands sharp as a shot, but measured, decorous, and the rest of us jumped to our feet in a great scrape of chairs and made the hall thunderous with applause and the rhythmic drumming of our feet on the oaken floor. Frost gave a little bow with his head but we kept up the racket and finally his reserve broke. He smiled boyishly and rose partway in his chair and waved his napkin at us like a flag of surrender.

I was conscious of him throughout the meal and held myself as though he were conscious of me. Some of the other boys at my table also suffered fits of dignity. The atmosphere in the hall had become theatrical. This had everything to do with Frost himself. The element of performance in his bearing—even the business with the napkin, awkward as it seemed, had a calculated quality—charged the room and put us on edge, not at all unpleasantly, as if a glamorous woman had entered the hall.

Frost read to us in the chapel that night. This was unique in my time at the school; the other visitors all spoke in the auditorium. Maybe it was a sign of the headmaster's special regard, or maybe Frost himself had asked to read there. Certainly it was the most beautiful building in the school, famous, we were often told, for its stained glass windows, plundered from France by some sharp alum. Even at night, weakly lit, the red panes glowed like rubies. The pews creaked as we settled in. We sat somberly in place, staring straight ahead or gawking up into the heights where the arched ceiling vanished in darkness. The iron chandeliers shed just enough light to cast long, medieval shadows and burnish the bronze memorial plaques, the rich woodwork, the plain gold cross on the altar.

Frost sat with the headmaster in front of the altar, hands on the carved armrests of his chair, his head bowed as if in meditation or prayer, but I was sitting near the front and I caught the gleam of his eye under the heavy white brows. He was watching us watch him. When the headmaster finally stood to make his introduction, Frost gave a start and looked around as if he'd been worlds away, and that finding himself here was a puzzle indeed.

The headmaster climbed the steps to the pulpit. He was a lanky, long-faced man with a big wen over his right eyebrow. It was a blistery-looking thing and when you first met him you could see nothing else, but he soon distracted you by holding your eyes with his keen, attentive gaze, and by the arresting beauty of his voice. He had a profound bass full of gravel, which he used to good effect and to his own satisfaction. When we made fun of him behind his back we forgot the bump and mimicked his rumbling drawl. *Purcell, you're not altogether a dull boy, perhaps you can explain what is meant by* peyote solidities, *or sexless* hydrogen . . . *I am trying to understand these words and I am failing, Purcell, I am failing.*

I expected the headmaster to use this moment for a swipe at the Ginsberg-Ferlinghetti crime family, which had a few soldiers among us, though not as many as he feared. He had read their work and affected to see no difference between "Howl" and "A Coney Island of the Mind." He did, of course. Ferlinghetti didn't really matter to him, but Ginsberg he hated. Though he disparaged him in aesthetic terms as sloppy and incoherent, what he really detested was his vision of America as a butcher of souls. The headmaster was a democrat and a meliorist. He'd been steadily adding to the number of scholarship boys, and we heard persistent rumors that he was badgering the trustees to lift the ban on black students. Perhaps he sensed in Ginsberg the herald of those descending furies that meliorism made only more rabid, that nothing could satisfy but the death of the imperfect republic whose promises he cherished, and tried to keep. He hid his detestation of Ginsberg in ridicule, quoting him with such simpering, deadly scorn—*Moloch in whom I sit lonely! Moloch in whom I dream Angels!*—that it took me many years to figure out that "Howl" was a great poem.

Whatever his reasons, he feared Ginsberg's influence on us to a degree that was almost respectful. Frost would serve as the perfect bludgeon. I caught Bill White's eye—we both knew what was coming.

But no. Instead the headmaster told a story of how, as a farm boy completely ignorant of poetry, he had idly picked up a teacher's copy of *North of Boston* and read a poem entitled "After Apple-Picking." He approached it, he said, in a surly humor. He'd done more than a bit of apple-picking himself and was sure this poem would make it fancy and romantic and get it all wrong. Yet what struck him first was how physically true the poem was, even down to that ache you get in the arch of your foot after standing on a ladder all day—and not only the ache but the lingering pressure of the rung. Then, once he'd assented to the details, he was drawn to the poem's more mysterious musings. What was that pane of ice about? Which part of the poem was dream, and which part memory? When he borrowed the book he'd had no idea where this act would lead him. Make no mistake, he said: a true piece of writing is a dangerous thing. It can change your life.

That was all. He came back down the steps. No recitation of Frost's honors and awards, no witty, polished reminiscences from the Amherst years. I had never before heard the headmaster speak of himself as someone with a particular past, and never did again; with us it was all books and ideas and what he liked to call, quoting Jane Austen, the compliment of rational opposition. He was married but hard to imagine in his wife's arms, because he seemed consecrated to a relationship with the world that yielded nothing to the flesh, whose unremitting satisfaction I conceived to be the point of marriage. He was a mystery to us and, like great generals and actresses, he guarded that mystery like the power it was.

He helped Frost up the winding steps and then, instead of returning to his chair, joined us in the pews. This left Frost alone at the front of the church, in the high pulpit. He arranged his books and some loose papers in a certain order, then rearranged them, the papers rustling loudly under the microphone. At this he stopped to inspect the mike as if the device were new to him. He tapped it suspiciously. This produced a resounding knock, and he shied back a little. He picked up a book, rifled through the pages, set it down again, and peered out at us.

Can you hear me? You can hear me, you boys in the back? Well then. Good. That's good. I suppose I should read you a poem. But I was just thinking about something Shelley said . . . you know Shelley, fellow who wrote "Ozymandias"—it's in your books. Friend of Byron, friend of Keats. Wife wrote *Frankenstein*. Anyhow, Shelley liked to say that we poets are the unacknowledged legislators of mankind. They used to speak like that in those days—by the pound. Unacknowledged legislators of mankind. Wonder if it's true. Wonder what it *means*. Does it mean we're dangerous, like your headmaster says? What does your man Kellogg think? Is Mr. Kellogg here tonight?

Frost waited, gazing out at us until George stood up, a couple of seats to my right. He looked furtive and damp. He looked like a sinner in a Last Judgment painting, about to get his due.

And Frost, Frost looked like Himself up there in the pulpit. He was standing below one of the chandeliers, whose wintry light silvered his hair and made shadows on his weathered face. He didn't look old; he looked eternal.

He took George in. So, he said. Mr. Kellogg. That was quite a piece of legislation you wrote. Bet you had some fun with it too, holding the old man's feet to the fire. Good for you, good for you.

Old men should have their feet held to the fire—keeps 'em awake.

All right, boys, they've brought me down here to sing for my supper, so I'd better do some singing. Here's one for you. No snow in here, Mr. Kellogg, but maybe we can find you some later on. I wrote this one when I was lonely for home, many years ago, in England. I expect you boys know about homesickness. It's called "Mending Wall."

He lowered his eyes to read and George wilted back into the pew.

> *Something there is that doesn't love a wall,*
> *That sends the frozen-ground-swell under it,*
> *And spills the upper boulders in the sun . . .*

He picked his way slowly through the first line, as if the thought were just occurring to him, and then his dry voice filled like a sail and became good-humored and natural and young. When his farmer said *Spring is the mischief in me* I smiled, because I'd already felt the mischief at work in him as he came alive in the warm day, carrying stones to the wall, watching his neighbor do the same, struck by the pointlessness of their labor and unable to resist teasing his neighbor about it. I had read the poem and thought I understood it: All walls should come down. But in Frost's voice the scene became newly vivid, and I caught something I'd missed; that for all the narrator's ironic superiority, the neighbor had his truth too. The image of him moving in the shadows *like an old-stone savage armed*—he himself was a good reason to have a wall, the living proof of his own argument that good fences make good neighbors. Maybe something doesn't like a wall, but take it down at your peril.

Frost was good at masking his eyes under those hanging brows, but now and then I saw him shift his gaze from the page to us without losing a word. He wasn't reading; he was reciting. He knew these poems by heart yet continued to make a show of reading them, even to the extent of pretending to lose his place or have trouble with the light.

His awkwardness took nothing from his poems. It removed them from the page and put them back in the voice, a speculative, sometimes cunning, sometimes faltering voice. In print, under his great name, they had the look of inevitability; in his voice you caught the hesitation and perplexity behind them, the sound of a man brooding them into being.

Frost read on, poem after poem, until the underclassmen began to cough and set their pews groaning. Then he raised his head and took us in. You boys are champion sitters, he said. You've got *Sitzfleisch*, as our great new friends the Germans would say. That's enough for one night, eh? Maybe just one more—what do you think—for your man Kellogg. Yes? All right then. I have just the poem here. I believe Mr. Kellogg knows it.

Still looking at us, Frost recited "Stopping by Woods on a Snowy Evening." Then he gathered his books and pages while we applauded. The headmaster went up the steps, conferred with Frost, came down again and raised his hand for silence. Mr. Frost, he said, had agreed to take a few questions, if we had any.

I had some. How did he know he was a good writer for all those years when nobody else knew? What did it feel like to write something really great? Why did he choose George's poem?

Sir, if I may . . .

I looked around. It was Mr. Ramsey. He was standing in his pew. Even in this dimness his chubby cheeks showed their youthful English bloom. Mrs. Ramsey was plucking at something on her sleeve. He had married her four years earlier right out of some southern women's college where he'd taught after leaving Oxford.

She was just a freshman at the time, and Mr. Ramsey lost his job and brought her north to Putney and then to us. Mrs. Ramsey worked in the library and never lacked for boys willing to help. She wore her honey-colored hair in long girlish braids, and smelled good, and her voice was low and pleasantly southern. She had a teasing manner, and looked at us as if she knew what we were thinking.

When they arrived, two years back, she was still in love with Mr. Ramsey. We could all see it. She hung on his voice, quoted his pronouncements. Lately this had changed. Since October I'd been assigned to their dinner table, and seen her look bored while Mr. Ramsey went on about something. On occasion she turned away while he was still talking and chatted with the boy next to her. She was easy to talk to.

Your work, sir, Mr. Ramsey said, follows a certain tradition. Not the tradition of Whitman, that most American of poets, but a more constrained, shall we say *formal* tradition, as in that last poem you read, "Stopping in Woods." I wonder—

" 'Stopping by Woods on a Snowy Evening,' " Frost said. He put both hands on the pulpit and peered at Mr. Ramsey.

Yes, sir. Now that particular poem is not unusual in your work for being written in stanza form, with iambic lines connected by rhyme.

Good for you, Frost said. They must be teaching you boys something here.

There was a great eruption of laughter, more caustic than jolly. Mr. Ramsey waited it out as Frost looked slyly around the chapel, the lord of misrule. He was not displeased by the havoc his mistake had caused, you could see that, and you had to wonder if it was a mistake at all. Finally he said, You had a question?

Yes, sir. The question is whether such a rigidly formal arrangement of language is adequate to express the modern consciousness. That is, should form give way to more spontaneous modes of expression, even at the cost of a certain disorder?

Modern consciousness, Frost said. What's that?

Ah! Good question, sir. Well—*very* roughly speaking, I would describe it as the mind's response to industrialization, the saturation propaganda of governments and advertisers, two world wars, the concentration camps, the dimming of faith by science, and of course the constant threat of nuclear annihilation. Surely these things have had an effect on us. Surely they have changed our thinking.

Surely nothing. Frost stared down at Mr. Ramsey.

If this *had* been the Last Judgment, Mr. Ramsey and his modern consciousness would've been in for a hot time of it. He couldn't have looked more alone, standing there.

Don't tell me about science, Frost said. I'm something of a scientist myself. Bet you didn't know that. Botany. You boys know what tropism is, it's what makes a plant grow toward the light. Everything aspires to the light. You don't have to chase down a fly to get rid of it—you just darken the room, leave a crack of light in a window, and out he goes. Works every time. We all have that instinct, that aspiration. Science can't—what was your word? *dim?*—science can't dim that. All science can do is turn out the false lights so the true light can get us home.

Mr. Ramsey began to say something, but Frost kept going.

So don't tell me about science, and don't tell me about war. I lost my nearest friend in the one they call the Great War. So did Achilles lose his friend in war, and Homer did no injustice to his grief by writing about it in dactylic hexameters. There've always been wars, and they've always been as foul as we could make them. It is very fine and pleasant to think ourselves the most put-upon folk in history—but then everyone has thought that from the beginning. It makes a grand excuse for all manner of laziness.

But about my friend. I wrote a poem for him. I still write poems
for him. Would you honor your own friend by putting words
down anyhow, just as they come to you—with no thought for the
sound they make, the meaning of their sound, the sound of their
meaning? Would that give a true account of the loss?

Frost had been looking right at Mr. Ramsey as he spoke. Now
he broke off and let his eyes roam over the room.

I am thinking of Achilles' grief, he said. That famous, terrible, grief. Let me tell you boys something. Such grief can *only* be
told in form. Maybe it only really exists in form. Form is everything. Without it you've got nothing but a stubbed-toe cry—
sincere, maybe, for what that's worth, but with no depth or carry.
No echo. You may have a grievance but you do not have grief,
and grievances are for petitions, not poetry. Does that answer
your question?

I'm not sure—but thank you for having a go at it.

You wouldn't have guessed, seeing Mr. Ramsey settle back
with a smile, that he'd just been stepped on by Robert Frost in
front of the whole school. He had been my fifth-form English
teacher and though I hadn't liked him I did find him interesting,
just as I'd found his question to Frost interesting. But many of his
students thought him a pseud for his high diction and his passion
for complicated European writers. They had surely enjoyed this
little show.

The headmaster led us in a last storm of applause, then we
filed out of the chapel into a hard freezing wind. I asked George
if he was headed to Blaine Hall, since it was rumored that Frost
might drop by there for a cup of mulled cider with the English
Club. No, George said—he was going back to his room.

Why? Scared he'll give you the business? He was just teasing
you, George.

He shook his head. Mr. Frost really thinks my poem is some kind of mockery of his work.

He's the one who chose it. If it bothered him, why would he do that?

I don't know why Mr. Frost chose my poem, he said. But he seems out of sorts about it.

What the hell. You can clear things up with him at your audience tomorrow.

If I have my audience.

What, you think he'll blow you off?

I didn't say that.

George. Hold up. Hold up!

We stopped on the path. The line of boys shuffled past us. A derelict kite flapped frantically in a tree. George looked away from me, back to the wind, tweed hat pulled low on his head. I think I'm coming down with something, he said.

George, you can't stand Robert Frost up.

It wouldn't count as standing him up if I was in the infirmary.

You chickenshit. You big baby.

George hunched deeper into his coat, hands jammed in the pockets.

You can't do this, I said. This is something special. Something to tell your kids about. Your grandkids!

He won't mind. He'll be glad.

George. George. This is really dumb. Where are you supposed to meet him, anyway?

Headmaster's parlor.

When?

After breakfast, George said, then turned and looked at me. Why?

Just wondered. Are you really going to back out?

I don't know.

What a waste.

We walked along to where the path forked. Come over to Blaine, I told him. We can talk it over.

He shook his head.

It'd be a complete waste if you backed out. I mean, he's *here*, George. Robert Frost. The chance of a lifetime. He's, what? Eighty-six? Eighty-seven? It's now or never.

I understand that.

So are you really backing out? Because if you are, there's no point in letting a chance like that go to waste.

I saw him begin to understand me. This has nothing to do with you, he said.

I'm just saying, why throw a chance like this away? He's willing to spend some time with one of us. If *you* won't meet with him, let somebody else.

Like you?

Sure. Why not.

You'd be willing to take my place?

Yes.

But he didn't choose your poem. He chose mine.

So? If you won't meet him, why not me?

Because you didn't win. I won. That's why not. Would you actually accept an honor you didn't earn?

Oh, like you *earned* it with those rhymes of yours? Please— we're not talking about *Paradise Lost* here.

George looked at me with cold curiosity. It unsettled me, but my blood was up and I couldn't stop myself. Would I accept a meeting with Robert Frost? I said. An *unearned* meeting, as opposed to an *earned* meeting, like yours? You bet your sweet ass I would.

George turned and started across the quad.

I followed. Are you backing out or not?

He didn't answer.

Wait'll he gets you alone, you big baby. He'll chop you into little pieces.

I stopped and watched him bend into the wind, coattails streaming.

Frost didn't turn up at Blaine Hall that night, but Mrs. Ramsey did. Her solitary entrance put everyone on alert, like a song going up an octave. Faculty wives didn't attend such gatherings without their husbands, and as adviser to the English Club Mr. Ramsey was supposed to serve as host. Mrs. Ramsey said he had a touch of the flu, and wanted her to stand in for him, and pay his respects should Robert Frost appear. I heard her tell this to some masters and their wives as she carried a plate of cookies around the crowded room. Then she said it to Bill White and me in the same words and with the same helpless shrug, pursing her lips in sympathy for her ailing husband.

Bill and I were standing by the fireplace. We each picked a cookie, and as she told her brave little lie Bill reached out and took the plate from her and set it on the mantel, below the picture of the Blaine Boys. She relaxed and made no move to go. I was struck by Bill's confidence. Somehow I didn't like it, but the result was fine—having Mrs. Ramsey linger with us.

She said she'd heard Frost read once before, when she was a student at Foxcroft, and afterward he'd met with the girls and talked about everything under the sun. He was very funny, which surprised her, though she supposed it shouldn't have, and a terrible flirt. Of course he got plenty of encouragement.

The heat from the fire brought a flush to her face and made her perfume thicker, headier. She turned to Mr. Rice, an English master and a southerner himself, who was tapping the ashes from his pipe into the fireplace. Do you think he'll come tonight? she asked.

Frost? I doubt it. He seemed pretty well played out by the end there.

Shoot, she said. She glanced toward the door as another group of boys came in, then turned toward Mr. Rice. Ramsey says y'all're bringing that Ayn Rand woman here.

Me—bringing Ayn Rand? What would Mrs. Rice say?

You know what I mean.

Bill and I looked at each other.

There may've been some talk about it, Mr. Rice said.

Oh, go on. It's true and you know it.

Roberta.

I know, I know, she said. Boys, you didn't hear a word. But still—Ayn Rand!

Honestly now, Roberta, have you read anything of hers?

Why, sure! Not a whole bunch. A little. A couple pages of one book, in a drugstore. I guess you'd have to say I haven't, really.

Nor have I, Mr. Rice said. And until I do I will refrain from poisoning these innocents against her.

I've read her, Bill said.

We all looked at him.

The discerning Mr. White! I am shocked, Mrs. Ramsey said, but I could see that she was amused by the coolness with which he claimed this dubious ground.

She has some interesting ideas, he said.

Just then some of the boys started to sing, and others chimed in, the masters and their wives looking on tenderly. When I first arrived here I had tried not to gape whenever a bunch of boys suddenly gave voice like this, on the bus coming home from a game, in a sound-swelling stone hallway. It was like being in a movie of some Viennese operetta where everybody in the hotel lobby bursts into song, the doorman in his field marshal's coat chiming in with a comical solo. Now I too knew the songs, and quickened to those moments when we leaned together, watching one another for cues, and joined our voices.

The singers began to gather around the fireplace. Mr. Rice gave way and drifted back toward the other masters, but Mrs. Ramsey stayed with us and was soon surrounded by the chorus we'd become. She swayed to the music, laughing softly at a witty stanza, closing her eyes at a romantic line. She didn't so much listen to the songs as receive them, as if we were serenading her. And indeed we were. She was a woman alone among us, eyes shining, color high, a pretty woman made beautiful by tribute of song. We could see our power to charm her and make her beautiful, and this gave boldness to our voices. All the poetry of the night, the agitating nearness of this young woman, the heat of the clove-scented room and the knowledge of the cold outside— all this was somehow to be heard in the songs we addressed to her. It was exciting and not quite proper, stirring and in some way illicit. It was a kind of ravishing. When one of the masters called a halt to it after several numbers—only as an afterthought pleading the lateness of the hour—we broke off as if coming out of a trance, hardly knowing where we were.

Mrs. Ramsey seemed a little dazed herself, and skittish. She collected some dirty cups and wandered back to the cider bowl, where I saw her in conversation with the Greek master's elderly wife. The next time I looked she was gone.

It was obvious that Frost wouldn't show. Still, I stayed until the end, even offered to help with the cleanup, but the wives stuffed my pockets with cookies and sent me packing.

After breakfast I chanced some demerits and skipped my warm, easy chore—helping sort that morning's mail—to join a crew of third formers who'd been assigned the job of rolling and lining the clay tennis courts overlooking the headmaster's garden. They glanced at me curiously but said nothing, these melancholy squirts with pallid faces hunched deep in the coats they were supposed to grow into. After a brief show of helping I broke off and stood by the fence, watching the garden. I kept my vigil for half an hour or so. No one came. I figured George had chickened out after all, the big baby.

But I was wrong. We walked to our dorm together after dinner that night—George couldn't hold a grudge—and he told me he'd spent over an hour alone with Frost in the headmaster's parlor. They'd started talking and never made it outside. Frost hadn't said much about George's poem, not in so many words, anyway, but he recited a few of his own and gave George some pointers. He also gave him an inscribed copy of his *Complete Poems*, and an invitation to drop by for a visit should he ever find himself in the neighborhood.

Ah, I said. Great.

We walked along. Then George said that Frost had left him with some advice.

What was that?

Do you know where Kamchatka is?

Not exactly. Alaska? Somewhere up there.

Mr. Frost told me I was wasting my time in school. He said I should go to Kamchatka. Or Brazil.

Kamchatka? Why Kamchatka? Why Brazil?

He didn't explain. He was going to, but then he had to leave.

Jesus. Kamchatka. *Kamchatka.*

Later that night I went to the library and looked it up. A peninsula in the remote far east of the Soviet Union, on the Bering Sea. Very few people lived there. It was dark half the year. They lived on the salted meat of salmon and also of bears, which greatly outnumbered the people and proved a sorrow to the unwary. When the taiga wasn't frozen over, it swarmed with biting insects. There were many volcanos and they were still active. The only picture in the Kamchatka entry showed two figures in parkas watching the top of a mountain being carried skyward on a fist of flame.

I closed the encyclopedia and sat listening to the wind rattle the mullioned panes behind me. What was it about Kamchatka, that a young writer should forsake his schooling to go there? Spectacle, maybe. The drama of strange people living strangely. Danger. All this could be good matter for stories and poems. But Frost himself had lived in New England all his life at no cost to his art, and I wondered if he'd ever even been there. I guessed not. But it meant something to him, Kamchatka, something to do with the writer's life, and what else could it mean but hardship? Solitude, darkness, and hardship. But he had also mentioned Brazil. I rose from my deep chair and crossed the room past boys dozing over books and exchanged the K volume for B.

ÜBERMENSCH

The rumor was true—Ayn Rand would be our next visiting writer. Some of the masters were sore enough about this to let the story of their failed protest sift down to steerage. It seemed that the chairman of the board of trustees, Hiram Dufresne, an admirer of Rand's novels, had insisted on the invitation. Mr. Dufresne was also very rich and rained money on the school—most recently the new science building and the Wardell Memorial Hockey Rink, named in honor of his roommate here, who'd been killed in the war. He visited often and liked to give the blessing before meals, serving up plenty of Thees and Thous and Thines; and afterward he would join us in Blaine Hall and lend his surprisingly high voice to the singing—a big, happy-looking man with an obvious orange hairpiece and a shiny round face and little square teeth like a baby's. He once stopped me on the quad to ask where I hailed from and how I liked the school, and as I gave my gushing answers he smiled and closed his eyes like a purring cat.

The headmaster invited Ayn Rand—so the story went—only because he was about to start a drive for scholarship funds and needed Mr. Dufresne's support. A small party of masters came to object, and Mr. Ramsey used an impertinent metaphor, at which point the headmaster blew up and sent them home with hard feelings against both him and Dean Makepeace, who'd taken his side. It was a measure of their resentment that these masters let us hear so much about this dispute.

Ayn Rand would visit in early February. By the time the announcement went out, just before Christmas break, I'd already heard the story behind it and was trying to figure out who held the high ground. Was the headmaster selling out, or were these masters indulging a mandarin snobbery regardless of the result? As a scholarship boy, I knew how I'd feel about losing my shot because some pedant wanted to show off his exquisite taste; but I was also affected by the masters' conviction that Ayn Rand simply did not belong in the company of Robert Frost or Katherine Anne Porter or Edmund Wilson or Edna St. Vincent Millay or any of the other visitors whose photographs hung in the foyer of Blaine Hall. The school, they believed, would lose no less than part of its soul by playing host to her, and to them the money made it even worse—*whoring after strange gods*, as Mr. Ramsey supposedly had put it.

By now I'd picked up enough swank to guess that Ayn Rand was as bad as she was popular, and she was very popular. In a smirky spirit I pulled a copy of *The Fountainhead* off a book rack in the train station as I was leaving for Christmas break, read a few pages for laughs, forgot to laugh, and got so caught up I decided to buy it. There was still a man ahead of me at the cash register when the conductor began his last call. The clerk was old and slow, damn his eyes. I stood there in a sweat, knowing I should give up and leave but unable to surrender the novel. In the end I made the train at a dead run, suitcases nearly wrenching my arms out of their sockets. But I had it—the fat book swinging in my raincoat pocket, banging against my thigh.

I was bound for Baltimore to spend the holidays with my

mother's father and his wife. The poky local was packed with boys from school, and on any other trip I would have been horsing around with the rest of them, but this time I found a nearly empty car and settled in with the novel. At the next stop down the line we took on a bunch of girls from Miss Cobb's Academy. I watched them milling around on the platform, waiting to board, and saw a girl I'd met at their Halloween dance. Her name was Lorraine—Rain, she called herself. By the third slow-dance we'd been pushing up close together, so close that one of the monitors wandering the floor tapped me on the shoulder with her pointer, which meant we had to retreat to opposite sides of the room and couldn't dance with each other again. Later I saw her making out with my classmate Jack Broome, which didn't stop me from writing her an ironically jocular letter a few days later. She never wrote back. Whenever I thought of that letter, as I often did, every phrase glowed with stupidity, made even more garish by the dead silence of its reception.

Rain came into my car, another girl at her elbow. Cigarette smoke curled from her nostrils. They stopped in the doorway and looked the car over. Her friend said something and Rain laughed, then she saw me and stopped. She was thrown. So was I. I had to force myself not to look away. A few weeks ago I'd been nudging a boner against her and she'd been sort of nudging back, the two of us holding this thing between us like an apple in some birthday game. Then she'd betrayed me and snubbed me. Now what?

I could see her decide to brazen it out. She said something to the other girl and came down the aisle, steadying herself on the seatbacks, long camel overcoat swaying to the rhythmic sideways lurch of the train. She was a redhead with beautifully arched eyebrows and pouty lips, her pale forehead faintly stippled with acne scars. When she talked to you she leaned back and narrowed her eyes as if sizing you up. She stopped beside me and asked where I was going, and when I said Baltimore she wondered if I knew some friend of hers who lived there.

I repeated the name thoughtfully, then said no, I didn't think I knew her.

Well, you should, Rain said. She's stupendous great fun. I'll tell her to look out for you.

Terrific.

She dropped her cigarette and ground it out, her leg flashing forward from the pleats of her skirt. She had on black stockings. Then she glanced back at her friend. Well, she said—Oh, don't tell me! She plucked the novel off my lap. Do not tell me you're reading this book!

It seemed useless to deny it.

She flipped through the pages, then stopped and began to read. Oh, God, she said, and went on reading long enough for her friend to look impatient. I waited, smiling idiotically. Dominique is my spirit guide, Rain said. You know what I mean?

Well, sure, I said. Absolutely.

Roark too, she said, but in a different way. I have a *completely* different thing with Roark. I'm not even going to try to describe that.

I know what you mean, I said, then added, Probably like what I have with Dominique.

Her friend called out and jerked her head toward the next car. Rain held the book out, then pulled it back. Can I borrow it? I don't have a *thing* to read.

No. Afraid not.

Please? Then, in a low voice: Pretty please?

No. Sorry.

She looked at me in that measuring way of hers. Maybe she was wondering whether I would take the book by force if I had to. She came up with the right answer. *Okay*, she said, and handed it over.

Rain hadn't bothered to close the book. I glanced over the pages she'd been reading and found this exchange between Dominique and Roark: *I want to be owned, not by a lover, but by an adversary who will destroy my victory over him, not with honorable blows, but with the touch of his body on mine. That is what I want of you, Roark. That is what I am. You wanted to hear it all. You've heard it. What do you wish to say now?*

Take off your clothes.

I read without stopping until we pulled into New York, where I took an empty bench in the station and went back to the book as my schoolmates played the fool around me. One boy had gotten plastered on the train and was puking into an ashtray, and a couple others were pretending to be drunk. What sheep!

It was dark when I boarded the train to Baltimore. Now and then I stopped reading to study my reflection in the window. *His face was like a law of nature—a thing one could not question, alter, or implore. It had high cheekbones over gaunt, hollow cheeks; gray eyes, cold and steady; a contemptuous mouth, shut tight, the mouth of an executioner or a saint.*

My cheeks weren't hollow and my eyes weren't gray, but my mouth surely tightened with contempt over the next weeks as I read and re-read *The Fountainhead* and considered how shabbily this world treats a man who is strong and great, simply *because* he's strong and great. A man like the architect Howard Roark, who refuses to change even one angle of a design to advance his career and who, when his finest work—a housing project—is secretly modified during construction, goes there and personally dynamites the whole thing to smithereens rather than let people live in such mongrelized spaces. His genius is not for sale. He is a free man among parasites who hate him and punish him with poverty and neglect. And he has sex with Dominique.

Dominique seems like a regular glacier as she rolls over the men in her path. With her *air of cold serenity* and her *exquisitely vicious mouth*, she treats Roark like dirt, talking tough to him, even smacking his face with a branch, but underneath she's dying for him and he knows it and one night he goes to her room and gives Dominique exactly what she wants, with her fighting him all the way, because part of what she wants is to be broken by Roark. *Taken*.

This was new and interesting to me—the idea that a woman's indifference, even her scorn, might be an invitation to go a few rounds. I felt like a sucker. It seemed that all my routine gallantries and attentions had marked me as a weakling, a slave.

I was discovering the force of my will. To read *The Fountainhead* was to feel this caged power, straining like a dammed-up river to break loose and crush every impediment to its free running. I understood that nothing stood between me and my greatest desires—nothing between me and greatness itself—but the temptation to doubt my will and bow to counsels of moderation, expedience, and conventional morality, and shrink into the long, slow death of respectability.

That was where the contempt came in. I had stayed with my grandfather and his wife on other vacations, and found them kindly but dull. Grandjohn was a retired air force colonel whose specialty had been photo analysis. While studying pictures of German trains during the war, he'd spotted a certain marking that led to an important bombing run. My mother told me that story. Grandjohn didn't tell stories. After the war he'd worked in an office at the Pentagon before getting put out to pasture. At first I'd attributed his blandness to a professional habit of secrecy, and made it romantic—monotony as cover.

This time, though, I watched Grandjohn and his wife with a cold eye. How could he have spent so many years in the air force without learning to fly? Thirty years around Mustangs and Tomcats and Saber Jets, and he seemed happy to pilot a desk to his retirement party.

Patty was his second wife, a friend of my grandmother's who'd married him after Grandmargie died. Patty was boring too. She read him the day's news while he peered at the crossword puzzle through his half-moon glasses. *They say they're going to widen the road where that car went off with all those kids.* She had covered the floors of their house in thick white carpets that deadened the air and made whatever you said in that woolen silence sound like the sudden caw of a crow on a damp day.

I began to feel their kindness as a form of aggression. Patty was pitilessly solicitous. I couldn't touch a book without getting grilled about the sufficiency of light and the comfort of the chair. Was I warm enough? Did I need a pillow for my back? How about one of the five thousand Cokes they'd stored up in anticipation of my visit? Grandjohn kept telling me how lucky I was to have my mother's eyes, and how proud of me she would have been. Sometimes I had to go into the bathroom and scream silently, rocking from side to side like a gorilla, my head thrown back, my teeth bared.

This, I decided, this sadistic dullness, this excruciating compulsion to please, was how you ended up after a lifetime of getting A's in obedience school. Roark had worked in a quarry, hewing granite blocks with a chisel, rather than take a job doing tame architecture. He refused to think as others would have him think. Had Grandjohn ever done anything else? Had Patty ever thought at all? Christ! How could they last another hour like this without cutting each other's throats?

I fled the house every chance I got, riding a bus the ten miles into Baltimore from Wilton Oaks, their housing development. It rained steadily through Christmas into the new year. I walked the glistening streets in a fury of derision, wet and cold, sneering at everyone except the drunkards and bums who'd at least had the guts not to buy into the sham. Despising any sign of uniformity, I saw uniforms everywhere—not only on soldiers and policemen, but on high school girls and housewives out shopping. The businessmen struck me as especially pathetic in their hats and suits and London Fogs, each with some laughable flag of individuality hanging from his neck.

The Fountainhead made me alert to the smallest surrenders of will. Passing a shoe store, I saw a young salesman in the act of bending over a customer's foot. I stopped by the window and stared at him, hoping he'd sense my rage and disgust. *You—is this your dream? To grovel before strangers, to stuff their corns and bunions into Hush Puppies? And for what—a roof overhead and three squares a day? Coward! Fool! Men were born to soar, and you have chosen to kneel!*

But he never looked my way. Instead he continued to chat up his customer, a grizzled old guy in overalls, all the while cradling the man's stockinged foot in one hand, examining it as if it were an object of interest and value. The salesman laughed at something the geezer said, then lowered the foot gently to the sizing stool. He rose and walked toward the back of the store. The old guy, smiling to himself, fingers laced across his stomach, stared past me into the street.

I returned to school three or four days before we were actually due back. Only a few boys were around, luckless scholars retaking tests they'd flunked, red-eyed swimmers tuning up for the season; otherwise the place was deserted. My reason for cutting the break short wasn't just to get away from Grandjohn and Patty. Our entries for the Ayn Rand competition were due the third week of January, and I wanted to get a jump on my story before classes started. But I wrote nothing. I took long walks through the snowy woods and fields, watching myself do it, admiring my solitude as if from a great height. Like Howard Roark,

I kept a cigarette clamped in my executioner's lips—once I got a safe distance from the campus—and between these bouts of passionate striding I pigged out with the jocks at the training table and lay on my bed reading *The Fountainhead* for the third time.

I wasn't writing, but that didn't trouble me—I knew I could deliver my story when the time came. What I was doing was tanking up on self-certainty, transfusing Roark's arrogant, steely spirit into my own. And as I read the book I could feel it happen, my sense of originality and power swelling as my mouth resumed its tightness of contempt.

For once I had a complete picture of the world: over here a few disdainful Roarks and a few icy Dominiques, meltable only by Roarks; over there a bunch of terrified nobodies running from their own possibilities. Now and then I caught glimpses of other ideas in the novel, political, philosophical ideas, but I didn't think them through. It was the personal meaning that had me in thrall—the promise of mastery achieved by doing exactly as I pleased.

When classes started I still hadn't begun my story; and the longer I went without writing, the more convinced I became of its inevitable superiority. By now I was reading *The Fountainhead* for the fourth time, my confidence at a boil as I fell behind in my assignments and picked up demerits for missing chapel and chores. Bill had to prod me to keep my side of the room halfway neat, and one afternoon he confiscated the novel and wouldn't give it back until I'd picked up the mess around my bed. Man, you're really hot on this stuff, aren't you?

She's good, I said. She's damned good.

She's okay.

Okay? Come on. I distinctly remember you saying how interesting she is.

I said she had some interesting ideas. Have you read her other book—*Atlas Shrugged?*

Not yet. I will.

It's all right, I guess. Same kind of thing. More speeches. Longer speeches. It kind of got on my nerves, actually—all that *Übermensch* stuff.

The German word shut me up. Our history master used it often—too often, really, and with excessive pleasure in his accent—to describe the Nazis' ideology. Because of this association, when Bill flashed the word I became instantly conscious of his Jewishness, and all the more so because he kept it to himself. I could have argued that a man with a mind of his own and a pair of balls to back it up didn't have to be a Nazi, but of course Bill hadn't actually said that. And something else made me hold my tongue. He knew that I'd caught on to his Jewishness, but he wasn't aware of mine, such as it was. I didn't want to say something that would touch so tender a nerve, a tenderness I assumed in him because I suffered from it myself, covertly bristling when I read or heard anything that might be construed as anti-Semitic. In fact that part of my blood felt most truly my own at just those moments when it seemed liable to condescension or ridicule. I figured Bill had kindred feelings, and I didn't want to provoke them by pushing a view that he identified with German murderers. Our balance was fragile enough anyway, with so many complications of ambition and envy and pretense.

The crowning irony was that Bill himself should appear so much the poster Aryan—so blond, so fair, so handsome. More than handsome: over the past months he had become beautiful. How had that happened? What had changed? Here, too, my secret knowledge of him cast a shadow, because what made him beautiful was a quality of melancholy that softened his gaze and the set of his mouth, and that I attributed to his Jewishness. It seemed to me that the other Jewish boys in school were subject to a similar poignance of expression—intermittently, of course, and some more than others, but all of them to a degree. It was one of the marks of their apartness.

As the submission deadline approached I entered a fever of elation, as if Ayn Rand had already chosen my story. I literally had chills, my brow was hot and clammy. I began to hear the voices of my characters and see their faces. It was all coming together: a great story, a masterpiece!

The day before it was due, without yet having committed a word of it to paper, I rose to read a passage of *L'Etranger* in my French class and my head kept floating up until it reached a zone of absolute silence and the faces turned toward me looked as featureless as plates of dough. Then my knees went watery and I reached out to steady myself but fell anyway, bringing my desk down with me. I was all tangled up in it. I tried to sit up and fell back again and lay there, waiting.

They kept me in the infirmary for almost two weeks. My fever was not, it turned out, the fizz of genius. It was influenza, complicated by walking pneumonia. Later, once he knew he wasn't going to lose me, the school doctor said that people had been dying of this particular bug and that I was lucky not to have died myself.

My dreams were so vivid those first few days that I could hardly tell waking from sleeping. The one thing I could be sure of was the constant presence of Grandjohn and Patty, who'd driven up from Baltimore right after the headmaster called them. They took turns at my bedside, sponging my face, helping the nurse feed me and change my sheets, supporting me on my wobbly, dizzying trips to the bathroom. Whenever I woke up, one of them was there. At first the sight of Patty or Grandjohn in the chair beside me made me weepy with gratitude, but as my head cleared I got tired of them and worried that they were imposing their dullness on the masters and boys who dropped by to say hello, and telling them more about me than I wanted known.

Then one morning the nurse brought in a box of chocolates with a tender farewell note from Patty and a copy of *Advise and Consent* Grandjohn had inscribed *To the budding writer*. The Colonel left these off for you, the nurse said. Didn't want to wake you up. Nice fella, the Colonel. Fine figure of a man.

I watched her set up my breakfast, a brisk, gum-chewing blonde with strong red hands. Her shoulder brushed mine as she cranked the bed upright, humming to herself, and I became aware of her as a woman. I knew my grandfather still made love to Patty. I'd heard their headboard banging the wall as I lay reading, and it embarrassed me, mostly for Patty's sake. She seemed too old for this—I thought of her as a victim in the transaction. But Grandjohn was still, as the nurse said, a fine figure of a man, tall and strong and jut-jawed, and I could sense his pleasure in the company of women. The nurse obviously had responded with pleasure of her own. I couldn't help thinking of their hours alone here among all these empty beds, the Nurse and the Colonel, and this thought—framed in that impersonal, tritely pornographic way—made me raw with suspicious envy. She must have caught it in my face because she gave me an amused, sidelong glance and flicked my shoulder with the napkin before dropping it in my lap.

That afternoon a third former who'd just been admitted to the infirmary told me that Purcell had won the audience with Ayn Rand. We were playing chess in the sunroom, and I bent low over the board so he couldn't see my face.

Not that I'd even submitted anything. Indeed, by now I could hardly remember the story I'd been so sure of. Most of it had vanished with the fever, leaving only traces of plot like the outlines in a coloring book. Since I couldn't have won, it followed that someone else would. So why not Purcell—talented, serious Purcell, Purcell who cared so much? Over the next few days I scraped together enough generosity to convince myself that I was happy for him, and when I got discharged the first thing I did was stop by his room to shake his hand.

What are you talking about? he said. I didn't win.

You didn't win? I heard you did.

Well, I didn't. Big Jeff won.

Big Jeff? *Big Jeff* won?

Purcell's roommate was all pretzeled over in a chair, cutting his toenails. He looked up and said, How's about *them* apples? Big Jeff, the award-winning author!

Purcell looked at him, and he laughed and went back to work with his clippers. They always acted like they hated each other, then signed up as roommates again every year.

I can't believe it, I said.

Purcell was lying on his bed. He lowered the book he'd been reading and stared up at the ceiling.

Jesus, I said. Big Jeff. Did you submit anything?

Yes, I have to admit I did. I actually put myself in the position of being judged by Ayn Rand.

Oh, bull. Have you even read her?

He didn't answer.

You haven't seen Big Jeff's story? the roommate said to me.

No. I've been sort of out of commission.

He looked at Purcell and smiled. It's a classic, he said. Schoolboys will be parsing its subtleties for generations to come.

Purcell closed his eyes.

So Big Jeff won, I said. Too much! I didn't know Big Jeff could write.

He can't, Purcell said.

Then why did she choose him?

He just shook his head, eyes still closed.

I'll tell you why, the roommate said. Because the blood of an artist runs in Big Jeff's veins. Because he's a two-fisted, bigger-than-life, award-winning author and not one of your local *artistes* who give themselves orgasms by forswearing capital letters and boring the living shit out of everybody. That's why.

He bent toward his desk and picked up a copy of the school paper. Here, he said. Read him and weep.

Big Jeff's story was called "The Day the Cows Came Home," and it managed to combine his vegetarianism with his interest in space travel.

It went like this. A flying saucer lands in a field outside Boston. The police and various armed services try to destroy it, without success. Then it fires a ray that atomizes a nearby truck, mercifully empty, and everyone backs off while an exhaustively described robot disembarks and demands that a delegation of world leaders present themselves to the saucer's commander. Tomorrow—or else.

Old hat so far, but not for long. The next day the president, the Soviet premier, and the queen of England assemble in the field and are led by the robot to the command center. And what do they find there, sitting at the controls and surrounded by a crew of the same species, but an enormous bull! This is no ordinary bull, but *a horned argonaut of imperial carriage* whose eyes *flash with preternatural intelligence* and who otherwise bears the same resemblance to earthly bovines that *the untrammeled wolf, bold ruler of his arctic realm, bears to the permed and coiffured poodle in his rhinestone sweater.*

Then the world's leaders get the story. Long ago, one of the aliens' ships had developed engine trouble and been directed to our planet because of its nutritious flora. Their own galaxy was light years away and by now the crew would've been dead for scores of centuries, but this expedition had come to gather the descendants of that valiant band and take them home. They *had* left descendants, hadn't they?

The perils of answering this question are not lost on the humans. They deny any knowledge of such creatures, until the ship's commander produces a picture of cows in a field—at which point the queen of England, *her tender female spirit unequal to the sternness of his gaze*, breaks down and babbles out the truth. The travelers gathered around her are not pleased to learn the present state of their kin, or the uses to which they've been put. Indeed they can hardly believe their ears, and the commander insists on a fact-finding tour.

He visits a dairy in Wisconsin, where he sees the cows sucked dry by machines and shot full of sperm from bulls they've never even met. He watches calves being castrated and branded in Texas, and tours a farm in Japan where the animals are force-fed gallons of beer to sweeten their flesh. He's taken to a messy bull-fight in Mexico, a rodeo in Wyoming, and a killing-floor in the Chicago stockyards.

The commander of the spaceship sees all this and more. He grows ominously silent. After returning to the ship to confer with his comrades, he emerges to make a grand tour of all the ranches and farms, gathering the herds around him to tell them exactly what lies in store if they don't accept his invitation to return to the home planet. They retain just enough of the old language to understand the warning, but most of them shrug it off. Instead they invite *him* to join *them*. They've got it made: all they can eat, protection from predators, medical care—the works. The commander is reviled as a troublemaker, and in Montana a bunch of steers stampede him off the ranch. Finally, only a handful of the bravest and smartest choose to leave, and even this small procession is diminished when some of them lose their nerve at the sight of the long ramp leading into the ship, and defect.

At sunset the saucer lifts off with its crew and their newfound cousins. But they don't head for home—not yet. They hang up there for a while putting their ray to work. The killing is efficient, implacable, and completely misanthropic. In the end not a single human being remains alive. The story concludes with this line, spoken by one of the crew to a cow weeping for the little boy who milked her: *He's lucky we didn't eat him.*

In her front-page interview, Ayn Rand praised Big Jeff as a great writer in the making. *It is most gratifying,* she said, *to see someone of Mr. Purcell's youth dare to challenge the collectivist orthodoxy that tyrannizes intellectual life in this country—and nowhere more than in its colleges and schools. Mr. Purcell excels in his depiction of the victim kissing the whip. Of course the herd denies the truth of its own enslaved condition, and attacks the heroic truth-teller. One need only read the reviews of Atlas Shrugged to see that principle at work in our so-called free press, which can appear free only to those who've been completely brainwashed by egalitarian mystifications. But just look what happens when truly superior men like John Galt cease to exercise their powers—the whole world comes to a halt!*

Ayn Rand spent most of the interview going on about this John Galt. Since I didn't know who he was I skipped to the end, where she came back to Big Jeff and complimented his use of the farm and the stockyard as a metaphor for the welfare state, *whose siren song lures us ever closer to the wasteland of coerced mediocrity—where to be done for matters more than to do, where freedom is a fantasy achieved by shutting one's eyes to the corral in which one lives, and where the herd counts itself fortunate to be fattened on the pro-*

ceeds of its own eventual slaughter. Mr. Purcell has here revealed a
great and most unpopular truth. The dream of universal equality leads
not to paradise, but to Auschwitz!

I couldn't shake the flu. My nose was red and swollen from
uncontrollable fits of honking, my eyes weepy, my upper lip
chapped. I dozed off constantly. Two days before Ayn Rand's visit
I was nudged awake by my Latin master and told, not unkindly,
to check myself back into the infirmary until I got well enough to
keep my eyes open in class.

Ayn Rand gave her talk in the afternoon. I'd thought of
sneaking out for it, but the nurse kept fussing through my room
and then I fell asleep and didn't wake up until Bill White dropped
by after it was over. He meant to cheer me up, of course, but
instead left me desolate for everything I'd missed.

He said that a bunch of Ayn Rand's followers had driven up
from Boston and waited over an hour in the snow—smoking like
chimneys, dropping their butts everywhere—so they could grab
the front seats. They looked like a bunch of undertakers, Bill said,
even the women, all of them silent and unsmiling in their dark
clothes. During the talk they applauded at odd times and generally made a stir.

But not as much as Ayn Rand. Right away she tore into our
school motto—*Give All*—and urged everyone to ignore such
drivel and live for themselves alone. Then she rebuked Hiram
Dufresne for calling her a conservative in his introduction. She
said that she was a *radical*, not a conservative, and that people
should attach meaning to the words they speak. Toward the end
some students actually walked out when she attacked President
Kennedy for inviting us to consider what we might do for our
country. Her talk went on too long for questions, but when the
headmaster suggested a follow-up meeting in Blaine Hall after

dinner, she agreed on the condition that only her *true readers* would be welcome—those who had read all her novels. She was willing to have a serious discussion, she said, but not to answer ignorant questions or be gawked at by tourists.

I came in at the last minute to give the masters less time to notice me and send me back to bed. There weren't many, as it happened—a young science master, another from history, the football coach, and Mr. Ramsey, who was officiating at the punch bowl, probably as penance for getting mouthy with the headmaster. Mrs. Ramsey stood beside him, talking to Big Jeff. Some fifteen boys were scattered around on folding chairs and an equal number of darkly dressed men and women—Bill's undertakers, no doubt—sat somberly in front of the fireplace. One of the women, a skinny thing with cropped blond hair, lit a cigarette, and when the football coach asked her to put it out she took another long drag and flicked it into the fire without even looking at him. The logs popped and hissed. Otherwise the room was eerily quiet.

Then Ayn Rand came in, accompanied by the headmaster and Hiram Dufresne and a tall, grave young guy with a pompadour. That she was short and blocky surprised me—I'd been expecting Dominique. Her dark hair was cut close, shaped like a helmet. She shrugged off her cape, handed it without a glance to the tall guy, and headed for the Morris chair that had been drawn up for her by the fireplace.

Mr. Dufresne began to follow but she turned toward him and said, quite distinctly, No further introduction will be necessary, thank you. Her voice was deep and richly accented. Mr. Dufresne stopped and blinked at her, then retreated to the side of the room.

Ayn Rand settled into the Morris chair and took a cigarette

from her bag and twisted it into a long black holder. One of the men in the front row leaned forward with a lighter. She bent toward the flame, then leaned back and looked us over, her wide red mouth fixed in a skeptical wince. She wore a black suit with a short skirt that rode up her thighs. She had nice legs for a woman so squarely built. A gold pin glittered on her lapel. The smoke from her cigarette drifted up past the picture of the Blaine Boys.

So, she said. How many writers have we among you boys?

The undertakers turned and looked at us. Not a single hand went up.

Come, come, she said. I know we have at least one, the estimable Mr. Jeffrey Purcell, whom I look forward to meeting. There must be others. No? Ah, your meek little hearts are afraid to show themselves. Shame on you! You must never be meek, the meek shall inherit nothing but a boot on the neck. You must be bold! My heroes have been ridiculed for refusing fear and compromise. My critics say such people do not exist. But allow me to inform you that I am such a person, and I most assuredly do exist!

She drew fiercely on her cigarette and leaned toward us. The light glanced off her gold lapel pin, which I now saw was a dollar sign.

In Russia, she said, as a student in Petrograd University, I studied by candlelight. There was no firewood, the ink froze in our pens. Mr. Lenin's altruists shot so many of us we had to rent the coffins in which we carried our teachers and friends to their graves. But I am still here. And why? Not because I kissed the rings of our new Russian popes, I assure you. Not because I gave in to fear. Never. To give in to fear is to be already dead. I refused fear, I refused defeat. Did you know that *The Fountainhead* was rejected twelve times? Imagine! But I did not accept defeat. That is why I am here, for that reason and no other. So please do not tell me that characters such as mine do not exist! No! She slapped the arm of her chair.

No! And please do not tell me that my characters are unreal because they live out their ideals. Of course the second-handers will tell you that the ideal is impossible, that a real story can only be a story of the folks next door, those frustrated imbeciles—a story of toad-eaters and mediocrities—a story of compromise and failure.

At that moment the sneeze I'd been trying to hold back exploded wetly. Ayn Rand fixed me with her dark, deep-set eyes as I wiped my raw lip and gave my nose a final clearing blast. She looked away only when a log collapsed heavily in the fireplace, sending up a flourish of sparks.

She contemplated the fire. Yes, she said. The folks next door. If you are not prepared to be vilified as I have been, you must take those drab little lives as your subject. The lives of *the people*. Of your *brother*. Remember this: when someone calls himself your brother, he does so with one desire—that you will become his *keeper*, a slave to his own incapacity and idleness. Above all, save yourselves from your brother.

Now, boys, here is a question for you. What does your value derive from? She watched us as she put another cigarette in her holder and accepted the flame from an outstretched hand. She let the silence grow. I noticed that her florid red lipstick was smeared at both corners of her mouth, and that a run in one of her stockings cut a long white scar across her knee.

Very well, she finally said. Let me tell you what your value does *not* derive from. It does not derive from the self-sacrifice demanded by some party, or state, or from the church of some ludicrous god. It does not proceed from the people. In exchange for your reason and your freedom they may give you a certificate of virtue, even some power, but this is worthless. It is less than worthless—it is bondage. When your power comes from others, on approval, you are their slave. Never sacrifice yourselves— never! Whoever urges you to self-sacrifice is worse than a common murderer, who at least cuts your throat himself, without persuading *you* to do it. You must revere yourselves. To revere yourself is to live truly. And as I know only too well, to live truly is to live at war. Yes, at war—with the *people* and the *party* and the guilt-peddling Jesus industry!

Hear, hear! barked a man in the front row.

Ayn Rand dipped her head in acknowledgment and gave a bitter smile. My heroes are impossible, they say. Unreal. And why do they say that? Because they want you to believe that heroism itself is unreal! They want you to despise yourselves before you discover what you're capable of. Boys! Please! You are born to be giants, not sacrifices to some tribal deity or some idiot fantasy of earthly paradise, or some brainless slattern worrying about the next payment on the refrigerator. What do other writers present as life? Little men and little women with little worries being held hostage by snot-nosed brats. They would have you think only this is real, that you must settle for this. The worst of lies! I say that what other writers present as life is nothing more than an alibi for cowardice and treason—treason against yourselves, against the John Galt in each of you.

I sneezed again. It had come on, strangely enough, at the mention of snot-nosed brats, and there was no stopping it. Ayn Rand stiffened visibly but didn't look at me.

Miss Rand?

She turned to face the headmaster. He was standing against the back wall, arms across his chest.

Miss Rand, you take a pretty dim view of your fellow writers.

She stared at him as if transfixed, perhaps by the wen on his forehead, which was glowing like a coal. Finally she said, Yes. What other view do they offer?

A good many, I think. But let me ask you this. If you had to name the single greatest work by an American author, what would it be?

Atlas Shrugged.

Your own novel.

Is there another?

And after that?

The Fountainhead.

Is there really no other American writer whose work you admire?

The ash on her cigarette, having grown to an improbable length, fell into her lap. She brushed it away, then glared at the gray smudge it left on her black skirt. There is one, she said. I am interested in the novels of Mr. Mickey Spillane. His metaphysic is perhaps rather instinctive but quite sound nevertheless.

Mickey Spillane? The mystery writer?

I would particularly recommend *I, the Jury.* In Mike Hammer he has created a true hero, one who doesn't torture himself in the current fashion with decadent niceties. Mike knows evil from good and destroys it without hesitation or regret. Most unusual. Most satisfying. I might also mention *Kiss Me, Deadly,* though Mr. Spillane leaves us hanging somewhat at the end. What will happen with Mike and the beautiful Velda? I believe he owes us a sequel.

I thought, What about Ernest Hemingway? and blurted the question in just those words.

Hemingway again! Hemingway with the beard! Please! What you find in Hemingway is everything that is wrong with the so-called literature of this country. Weak premises. Weak, defeated people. A completely malevolent sense of life. Why should that nurse, what's her name, *Catherine*—why should Catherine have to die at the end? No reason. Only to give the lieutenant a tragedy to excuse his self-pity. Unreadable mush! And I understand that the other novels are even worse. Indeed, I'm told that one of them has a hero with no—how shall we say this—no *manhood*. How fitting! And what shall we learn from this wretched eunuch to whom the great bearded Ernest Hemingway has devoted an entire novel? The superior virtue of impotence? No thank you!

At this she looked from me to the headmaster, ignoring the laughter and applause from her chorus.

But it was Hiram Dufresne who spoke next. I read that book, he said. A long time ago, but I still remember it. That's a war injury you're talking about.

I don't claim to know, she said.

Well, my point is, Miss Rand, you were talking about heroism here, and to my way of thinking a war injury is more likely a sign of heroism than weakness.

She shrugged. That depends. If the wound is received through an action undertaken for the happiness of the man himself, it might be heroic. If for the sake of others, as self-sacrifice, I would call it weakness.

I don't know that any man is glad to die in a war.

Then he should choose not to. He has a sovereign right to seek his own happiness in his own way, short of violating the rights of another man. You've read John Galt's speech, I assume. It's all there.

That *sounds* fine, Miss Rand, but the truth is you only get to say it because so many good men died fighting. I knew some of them.

Please—you're confusing the question. The question is, what was their motive? If they died fighting for their own happiness, they have my respect. If they sacrificed themselves for mine, they died weakly and, I should add, irrationally, even immorally. If to *die* for the so-called public interest is good, if the public interest is the moral validation of an act, then it must also be good to bully and rob and sacrifice others for the public interest. Then you have justified the fascism of a Hitler or a Kennedy. Yes, Kennedy! Now, sir—you are an industrialist, are you not?

Mr. Dufresne was slow to answer. Though looking at her, he appeared to be lost in his own thoughts. Yes, he said, I have a number of concerns here and abroad.

I trust you do business for your own benefit, not as a public service.

Actually, Miss Rand, I do think of my work as benefiting others. It's what keeps me going. This'll sound pretty corny, but I want to give back what I've been given. I've been given a lot, as I'm sure you have.

Then you are sure of an untruth. I've been given nothing. And I have no doubt that you exaggerate your own debt, as you've been so carefully taught to do. I have always said that the only thing wrong with the American industrialist is his innocence. He has no idea what this country owes him. On the contrary, he accepts the shame forced on him by the very parasites who would suck him dry. Poor baby, he even seeks their blessing! But here . . .

She uncrossed her legs and drew herself erect. Here, she said, is a true blessing for you, in the name of the Individual, Capitalism, and the Spirit of John Galt. And with her cigarette holder she traced a figure in the air—a dollar sign.

Hiram Dufresne started to reply but broke off when a man in the front began clapping. His companions joined in. The skinny blonde stood and, when the applause died down, said in a trembling voice, Miss Rand, I just want you to know that your books have completely changed my life.

As they should, dear, as they should. Ah, I see my guardian angel pointing at his watch. Is there a last question?

A boy named Jaspers had been waving his arm like a railroad switchman, but just then Mrs. Ramsey raised her soft southern voice from the back of the room. We all make mistakes, she said. If this isn't too personal, Miss Rand, what was the biggest mistake you have ever made?

I reject your premise. If you act rationally, you cannot act mistakenly, and I have always acted rationally.

Jaspers started to wave again, but Big Jeff was already on his feet. Miss Rand, your books reach thousands of people—

Millions.

Millions of people. Just think what a difference it would make if they knew your position on meat.

She bent forward. *What?* What is it you're saying?

Just that if your readers knew you didn't eat meat, I bet a lot of them would give it up too.

Meat? She pushed herself up from the chair. Are you talking about *meat?* What depraved psychology prompts you to speak like this to the author of *Atlas Shrugged?*

This is our own Jeffrey Purcell, the headmaster said. As it was his story you chose, perhaps Jeffrey can be forgiven for thinking you agreed with his thesis.

Meat? She flapped her hand in front of her face. Enough, she said. I am quite finished.

The tall fellow came up with her cape and settled it on her shoulders as the admirers surged forward and the rest of us stood and stretched and began putting on our coats. All of us but one. Still waving his arm, Jaspers finally cried out, Miss Rand! Miss Rand! The room went quiet and she looked at Jaspers and he asked the question he'd been dying to ask. She jerked her head back as if she'd been slapped. All the dark-dressed men and women turned on him in utter loathing—a court of ravens about to eat the eyes out of this whey-faced, homesick boy with his chewed-up fingernails and puppyish need to be in on everything, who in his need had asked Ayn Rand the very question I had been itching to ask and probably would've asked if she hadn't skunked me for mentioning Hemingway.

Who is John Galt?

SLICE OF LIFE

Who is John Galt?

By a joke of fate, the question that brought poor Jaspers into such disfavor turned out to be the very first line of *Atlas Shrugged*, as I discovered when I borrowed the book from our library a few days after Ayn Rand's visit. I took a few runs at it but never got past the opening chapter. And when I returned to *The Fountainhead* I couldn't read that either, not anymore.

The problem was that I could no longer read Ayn Rand's sentences without hearing her voice. And hearing her voice, I saw her face; to be exact, the face she'd turned on me when I sneezed. Her disgust had power. This was no girlish shudder, this was spiritual disgust, and it forced on me a vision of the poor specimen under scrutiny, chapped lips, damp white face, rheumy eyes and all. She made me feel that to be sick was contemptible. There couldn't have been any other reason for her to despise me so, not at that moment, before I'd offended her by mentioning Hemingway.

At first I wondered if I'd mistaken her expression, but she snuffed that small doubt with the look she gave our headmaster. Her revulsion was as naked as a child's, and it continued to show itself in the cold, offended tone she used with him. It seemed that a wen was no less damnable than a runny nose. And this alone made it hard for me to read even the novel I'd been so captured by. I became touchily aware that both Roark and Dominique looked great and never had a sick day between them. Before now I'd taken their good looks for granted, like the ugliness of their archenemy Ellsworth Toohey. It hadn't occurred to me that the author actually thought that an afflicted face was deserving of scorn.

Her heroes were hearty, happily formed, and didn't have brats. In fact there were no brats at all in *The Fountainhead*, or in what little I read of *Atlas Shrugged*. The heroic life apparently left no time for children, or domestic cares, or the exertions of ordinary sympathy. After getting pinned by her look I couldn't imagine Ayn Rand driving eight minutes, let alone eight hours, to nurse a sick relative. The same went for Dominique and Roark, who seemed to have no relatives, or even friends—only inferiors. For several weeks I'd measured other people against them, and other people had always come up short. Now I couldn't read the novel without trying to imagine the two of them changing my sour sheets, walking me to the can. No dice. They wouldn't have lasted five minutes in that sickroom. They wouldn't have shown up at all.

The self-pity I felt at this betrayal dressed itself up as fierce affection for Grandjohn and Patty, who *had* done all this for me. I found myself defending them against Dominique and Roark as if they, not I, had turned up their noses at these loyal, goodhearted bores. And this line of thinking led me back to my own home, which Ayn Rand would consider a perfect instance of the drab little life she'd condemned. My mother had certainly been held hostage by one snot-nosed brat. Too much of her short life had been lost to worries about lousy cars, lousy teeth, lousy *refrig-*

erators. And as for my father, his already uncertain character devastated by grief, God knows there was plenty of weakness there.

That much was true. But Ayn Rand's cartoon vision of my parents—*brainless slattern, frustrated imbecile*—sickened me. She had no idea what went on between such beleaguered people, how infinitely complicated it was and dramatic, the effort it had taken them to keep going through all the disappointment and sickness and dreams of escape. I blamed Ayn Rand for disregarding all this. And I no doubt blamed her even more because I had disregarded it myself—because for years now I had hidden my family in calculated silences and vague hints and dodges, suggesting another family in its place. The untruth of my position had given me an obscure, chronic sense of embarrassment, yet since I hadn't outright lied I could still blind myself to its cause. Unacknowledged shame enters the world as anger; I naturally turned mine against the snobbery of others, in the present case Ayn Rand.

This part of my reaction was personal and unreasoned. But there was more. It had dawned on me that I didn't really know anyone like Roark or Dominique. Though Ayn Rand insisted that such people existed and that she herself was one, my own experience of them was purely literary. Everyone I knew, even in the most privileged families, was beset by unheroic worries. A brilliant daughter made pregnant by her piano teacher, a sweet-tempered son gone surly and secretive, flunking out of school and shedding his friends and wrecking one car after another as if with a will; nervous breakdowns and squabbles over money. I had stayed with these families during holidays and long weekends, and among even the happiest of them I had learned to efface my presence at certain moments—the sound of a door slamming upstairs, a husband's dark silence as his wife poured herself yet another glass of wine.

The people I knew, and the families I knew, were all more or less beset. And none of them—not one—seemed capable of the perfect rationality and indomitable exercise of will that Ayn Rand demanded as a condition of respect. Nor, I had to admit, was I. Everyone was troubled, nobody measured up, and I began to think that the true failure lay in Ayn Rand's grasp of human reality.

Her ridicule of Hemingway brought this home to me. Not immediately, of course. My first reaction was shock—at her unfairness not only to the writer but to a character for whom I had a great liking. Wretched eunuch, she'd called Jake Barnes, as if the fact of such a wound, of woundedness itself, made him merely pathetic. I knew Jake pretty well, having read *The Sun Also Rises* twice the previous summer. He'd gotten about the worst break I could then imagine, but he wasn't wretched. He took pleasure in how Paris came to life in the morning. Pleasure in food and drink and travel, in watching men face dangerous animals, in fishing, in friendship. Jake lingered on these things. He watched the life around him with interest. You could sometimes feel the pulse of hopeless longing, but you could not say that Jake was wretched. It was wrong, and it was mean.

It had become a fashion at school to draw lines between certain writers, as if to like one meant you couldn't like the other. So far I'd avoided the practice. I liked most of what I chose to read and saw no point in reducing my pleasures by half. But Ayn Rand jolted me into taking sides. She made me feel the difference between a writer who despised woundedness and one for whom it was a bedrock fact of life.

In the weeks after her visit I re-read *In Our Time* and all the Hemingway stories in my textbooks and anthologies. The young narrator of "In Another Country" has been shot in the leg, and among his crowd of patients he's the lucky one. Manolo in "The Undefeated" goes straight from a hospital bed into the bull ring and is almost immediately gored again. "The Battler" opens with Nick nursing a black eye, just before he meets a punch-drunk boxer with one ear gone and the other worn to a nub, and in "Cross-Country Snow" he can't telemark because of a wound to his leg. The narrator of "The Snows of Kilimanjaro" is dying of gangrene. All these wounds and scars . . . I'd never linked them up before, but when I did they began to seem the most visible symptoms of a general condition that included the Swede's despair, Francis Macomber's humiliation, Krebs's inability to feel.

There's a moment at the end of "Indian Camp" when Nick's father is rowing them home after delivering a baby by cesarean. It's been a rough morning. In the course of the birthing the baby's father, unable to leave the hut because of a crippling axe wound, was driven to such distress by his woman's cries that he slashed his own throat. Nick avoided watching the operation, but had a good look at the dead man's neck when his father examined the cut. He's young—still calls his father Daddy. Now they're crossing the lake toward home, Nick trailing his hand in the water. And what is he feeling?

In the early morning sitting in the stern of the boat with his father rowing, he felt quite sure that he would never die.

I first read the end of this story with something like nostalgia. What child hasn't dreamily trailed a hand in the water, lulled by the creak of oars in stronger hands, the rhythmic lunge of the boat? This memory, more the body's than the mind's, brought with it a recollection of the old serene trust that the world was kindly and mine for good. I recalled having this trust, and so recognized what Nick was feeling, but I no longer felt it myself.

It had a sting in its tail, this quiet passage. Even as I smiled at young Nick's doomed assurance—doomed the instant he insisted on it—I understood that mine was already gone, and with it the trick of not seeing my own fate in that of others. At this moment

I knew what I knew: that what happened to everyone else would happen to me.

You can't read "Indian Camp" and then go back to *The Fountainhead*. Everything seems bloated and cheesy—the swollen sentences, the hysterical partisanship of the author, the crassly symbolic, uninflected characters, the impossible things they think and say and do. Really, you can't believe a word of it. "Indian Camp" ruined *The Fountainhead* for me, even as the novel helped me to see the patience and delicacy and adamant reality of the story.

I already admired Hemingway above all other writers, but the truth was that I'd been drawn to him mostly by his life—that is, by the legend of his life—and by a set of ideas about his work that spilled over from the legend. I'd gone in looking for images of toughness, self-sufficiency, freedom from the hobbles of family and class and conventional work, so that's what I'd found. Now I was reading a different writer. Hard things happened in these stories, but the people weren't hard. They felt the blows. Some of them gave up and some came back for more, but coming back wasn't easy. The first time I read "Big Two-Hearted River" I liked it for its physical details. You saw everything Nick did, in precise, almost fussy descriptions that most writers would've left out. How he drives the pegs of his tent until the rope loops are buried, and holds his pants and shoes in his hand when leaving the tent at sunup. How he dampens his fishing leaders. Exactly how much flour and water he uses to make his pancakes—a cup of each. I'd liked being in on all these rough solemnities but I had missed the fact that Nick observes them so carefully—religiously is not too strong a word—because they keep him from falling apart.

How had I missed that? Reading the story now, I saw everything through the shimmer of Nick's fragility.

We had been taught not to confuse the writer with the work, but I couldn't separate my picture of Nick from my picture of

Hemingway. And I had a sense that I wasn't really supposed to, that a certain confusion of author and character was intended. But the man who lived in these stories was not the steely warrior-genius whose image had so fogged my first impressions. He was in most respects an unremarkable, even banal man who got things wrong and suffered from nervousness and fear, fear even of the workings of his own mind, and who sometimes didn't know how to behave. I hated the way he dumped Marjorie in "The End of Something." Telling a girl whose love you'd taken advantage of that it wasn't *fun* anymore? I judged him for that, thinking how much better I would've handled it.

I judged him, but I also understood that he'd allowed me to, and this was chastening. Knowing that readers like me would see him in Nick, he had given us a vision of spiritual muddle and exhaustion almost embarrassing in its intimacy. The truth of these stories didn't come as a set of theories. You felt it on the back of your neck.

Not everyone at our school loved Hemingway; he had his critics. One of our English masters, Mr. Rice, a native of Mississippi, insisted on putting him in the ring with Faulkner. At dinner it was sometimes his pleasure to recite the infamous love scene from *For Whom the Bell Tolls*, flattening his rich drawl into a deadpan that threw every fault of sentiment and phrasing into painful relief. One night I tried to return the fun with a passage from *Absalom, Absalom!* that I had memorized for this very purpose. Blowing my voice into a fat bubble of molasses, thus did I answer his Hemingway with my Faulkner: . . . *talking in that grim haggard amazed voice until at last listening would renege and hearing-sense self-confound and the long-dead object of her impotent yet indomitable frustration would appear, as though by outraged recapitulation evoked, inattentive and harmless, out of the biding and dreamy and victorious dust.*

I was enjoying myself so hugely that I failed to notice the ice thickening on the table, but when I brought the passage home nobody laughed. All the boys were tending fixedly to their meatloaf. Only Mr. Rice was looking at me, over the rim of his glasses, and I understood the instant I met his gaze that but for the luck of age and circumstance I might well find myself called out to an affair of honor. Finally, as if not trusting himself to speak to me, he turned savagely on the boy to his right and said, You will be so good as to pass the catsup, sir!

I knew there was a vein of portentousness and swagger in Hemingway; mimicking it was good sport even among those of us who looked up to him. But I did look up to him, now more than ever. So much, in fact, that I began to copy out his stories. I'd read an article about a writer's colony in Marshall, Illinois, where the aspirants spent their mornings transcribing masterworks in order to learn what it actually *felt* like to write something great. James Jones had been associated with this group. If the practice helped him write *From Here to Eternity*, why couldn't it help me? I used my typewriter because Hemingway famously did—posed above it in a photo over my desk—but I slowed myself to hunt-and-peck speed so I could feel the sentences take form, sense the shift in focus or tone when I struck the carriage return for a new paragraph; a thoughtful pause as I read over the page I'd just finished and slowly rolled a fresh one onto the platen, then the final period smacking home and all the joy of completion, the joy of Hemingway himself, as I rolled out the last sheet of "The Undefeated," laid it upon the others, and squared the stack.

None of this seemed ridiculous to me. A friend's parents back home had learned complicated dances by following footprints on diagrams they rolled out on the floor. I'd seen them do the mambo very impressively at a Christmas party, and they sure as hell weren't using their scrolls. They weren't even watching their feet. They were just doing what came naturally, from instincts they had trained with certain devotions, and the result was invention, freedom—mambo!

I had written "Indian Camp" and "The Undefeated" and had just begun "The Killers" when the headmaster remained standing after the dinner blessing one night and announced that Ernest Hemingway had agreed to be the next visiting writer. He would be with us in the middle of May, some six weeks hence. The headmaster watched us, enjoying the shock he'd produced. I glanced over at Dean Makepeace; he had to be behind this visit. Other boys were looking at him too. He was bent forward in his chair, studying the tablecloth. Then someone yelled *Bravo!* and the room went nuts—whistles, shouts, feet drumming the floor, fists pounding the tables. It started to die down, then flared up again. None of the masters tried to stop it. They couldn't have. It was about Hemingway, sure, but it was also about the sap starting to run after the first warm week since Thanksgiving. But mostly it was about Hemingway, and at that moment sitting in the dining hall surrounded by cheering boys, I felt quite sure my story would win.

THE FORKED
TONGUE

That was the sweetest spring of all my years there. An early shock of heat forced the leaves and blossoms to a lushness that came to seem downright tropical when the chemistry master's parrot escaped into an elm overlooking the quad. There he preened his bright feathers and stridently mocked us until starvation humbled him to earth, where he sold his freedom for a groundsman's peanut butter sandwich. The sudden departure of Roberta Ramsey darkened the campus for a few days; she simply vanished, and Mr. Ramsey's gloom was all the explanation we had. But the sap was running, and for the rest of us the shadow passed.

Mr. Ramsey had once told us about a riot of boys at his old school, Winchester, back in 1793, that finally had to be put down by a regiment of dragoons. In pale midwinter, with each of us hunched over his own faint ember while the latest blizzard howled at the windows, this story had seemed remote and improbable. Not now. We were all a little drunk with spring, like the fat bees reeling from flower to flower, and a strange insurrectionary current ran among us.

This went beyond the usual swagger of bloods about to graduate. Even small fry still in beanies started showing up late to class, went sockless in their loafers, forgot to say Sir and then paused a near-defiant beat when invited to correct themselves. The masters chose to regard most of these provocations as trivial, even ludicrous, like the grousing of impotent peasants outside the castle walls. They felt the season too; it softened them. And the last thing they wanted was to throw out a boy from my class, so close to the finish line. We really had to force their hand, and we did, three times.

It wasn't mutiny that caused the first expulsion. You might say it was the opposite—excess of devotion. When our glee club went to Boston to sing at an alumni dinner, a boy named Keyes filched a bottle of champagne and got sloppy, maudlin drunk on the bus ride back to school. Some of the other choristers, myself among them, managed to hustle him up to his room undetected, but once there we couldn't keep him quiet. He was bawling the school songs, hanging all over us and telling us what great guys we were and how we should start some kind of club together.

The hall master took his time in coming. When he finally showed up he simply tapped on the door and told us to call it a night. He obviously didn't want to see anything that would make him take action. Then Keyes broke loose and crashed into the hallway and threw his arms around the master, slobbering school spirit. Other boys came out of their rooms to see what was going on. The master gazed at us from Keyes's embrace. You could tell by how sad he looked, how resigned, that Keyes was a goner.

Then Jack Broome, Handsome Jack himself, Backfield Jack, Captain of Everything, got bounced for hitchhiking down to Miss Cobb's Academy one night to meet a girl. When they caught them in the boathouse there it was curtains for her, and our headmaster could do no less.

Not long after this my friend Purcell began to cut daily chapel. He simply, steadfastly, would not go, and I was only one

of many who tried to get him to relent before they had to kick
him out. Purcell refused. He said that God was just a character in
a Hebrew novel and if it came to that he'd rather worship Huck-
leberry Finn. Really, he said, I don't believe a word of that stuff.

You don't have to.

You don't have to, maybe.

It's what, fifteen minutes a day? It doesn't have to mean anything you don't want it to mean. Think your own thoughts.
What's the harm in that?

Just going through the door makes me a liar, Purcell said. I'm
not going to do it again.

He meant what he said. I kept my counsel when I saw the
pleasure Purcell took in rejecting it: saw that it made him feel
honorable in comparison to me.

We were allowed a fair number of cuts, but by the end of
April he'd used his up and the demerit meter was ticking. The
rest of us looked on with a murmurous show of dread as his tally
climbed toward the sudden-death number, and told one another
how much we admired him for sticking to his guns. And I did,
somewhat, though my admiration was muddied by Purcell's taking the high road with me, as if my going to chapel was nothing
but show.

The truth was that I looked forward to the moment each day
when I passed through that limestone arch he so abhorred. We
were loud boys, forever bellowing and jeering, yet we all knew to
shut up when we entered the chapel. You felt the hush there as a
profound agreement, an act of three hundred wills, and that made
it even deeper and more calming. The chaplain always did a short
reading and led us in a couple of hymns, but we were otherwise
left to the silence and the dark wood, the glowing windows and
rough stone and dim vaulted spaces overhead. Purcell ridiculed
even the architecture—Episcopalian English-envy, he called it—

which irritated me. I didn't like to wonder if my responsiveness was only another kind of snobbery.

But it was Purcell's crack about the Hebrew novel that really rubbed me wrong. Not the glib irreverence, but the way he said *Hebrew*. It came to me as a rank, dismal breath from some deep well of genteel disdain. Purcell didn't mean it like that, and he would've hated the notion of speaking with the unconscious voice of his class. That made it all the worse; it was so unconscious and therefore incorrigible an assertion of class that it made me feel a kind of despair. I wanted to say, *Don't you know who you're talking to?* But of course he didn't know. I'd made sure of that.

As the days passed I came to see the drama of his refusal as another display of blood-borne assurance. It mattered very much to me that I graduate, whereas it didn't really matter to Purcell. A diploma from the school would open no doors to him that weren't already open just because he was his father's son. He wouldn't even lose his place at Yale. Unless you got kicked out for an Honor Code violation, you could still take final exams at the end of the year and the school would certify that you had met its academic requirements.

What Purcell would actually lose, then, or renounce, was the chance to end this span of years and shared life with the rest of us. To sit with us on the graduation platform and feel silly in his mortarboard cap and mutter dark footnotes during the As-you-go-forth speech. Then to mingle on the quad with our proud families, drifting from group to group, shaking hands, putting on his best manners with those most obviously not of his world. To doctor his punch from a friend's flask, but only once, not wanting to dull himself to the unexpected full-heartedness he feels. To linger as the shadows spill across the grass and day turns to dusk—even to lend his raspy voice to the songs being raised by boys still not ready to say good-bye to each other. To look into their faces, some dear, some not, all of them familiar as his own, and allow himself a moment's blindness as our last song dies away.

I'm sure I was not alone in having imagined this day ever since I came to the school. But Purcell could give it up without a backward glance because to him the years now closing were a story of no importance, if a story at all. He instinctively saw himself as belonging to a narrative so grand that this part of it counted only as transitional material.

So I suspected. Or, to put it another way, I suspected that his willingness to be expelled was less a proof of principle than a sort of colossal snub.

And there was something else. Purcell had begun to absent himself from chapel as the stir over Hemingway's visit grew more and more feverish. The English masters were all teaching his work. The art master had produced a striking poster—the famous face suggested by a few black strokes over the line *One must, above all, endure*—that stared out from every bulletin board and entryway. Knowing that the greatest of living writers would soon be among us made us a little crazy with self-importance. Nor was it just the literary boys who got worked up; it seemed like most of the class planned to enter a story. As Picasso and Ted Williams knew Hemingway, as *Kennedy* knew Hemingway, one of us would soon know Hemingway and so be raised to that company.

Purcell loved Hemingway's work. He surely wanted that private audience as much as anybody, but I knew he hated the idea of competing for it. So did I. Only one of the many could be chosen, we all understood that, yet you couldn't help feeling that not to be chosen was to be rejected. And to be rejected by Ernest Hemingway—Ernest Hemingway tossing your story aside, *No, not him, not a prayer*. What a terrible thought! If being chosen was a blessing (and how else could you see it?) then to be rejected was a curse. That's how the logic worked for me. I assumed it worked the same way for Purcell, whose vanity was at least as wary of rebuke as my own.

Submissions were due the first Monday in May, two weeks before Hemingway's visit. If Purcell kept cutting chapel, his demerits would send him home on the preceding Saturday. He'd lose his chance for the audience, but spare himself the indignity of jostling with the herd and quite possibly losing. Yet in the very act of retreat he would seem a hero, the boy who would not falsely bend his knee. His expulsion would pass into legend.

I never thought Purcell had planned any of this, or that he was aware of any fault line under his resolve. He no doubt took his motives at face value. I didn't, that was all.

But I might have been wrong. And if I was wrong, supposing so much doubleness in Purcell, it was probably because I saw so much in myself. I should have been rejoicing. I'd been awarded a full scholarship to Columbia University, *to work with Lionel Trilling*, as I liked to think, and often told myself. An essay I'd written on Shakespeare's Sonnet #29—*When in disgrace with Fortune and men's eyes*—had just won the Cassidy English Prize, a great stroke of luck: five weeks at a summer program in Oxford, all expenses paid. My classmates liked me, most of them, and a few of the younger boys paid me a kind of puppyish attention that I recognized from my own early days, when some upperclassman caught my eye.

And why would I catch a new boy's eye? Maybe because from my own anxious studies I had made myself the picture of careless gentility, ironically cordial when not distracted, hair precisely unkempt, shoes down at heel, clothes rumpled and frayed to perfection. This was the sort of figure I'd been drawn to almost from the beginning; it had somehow suggested sailing expertise,

Christmas in St. Anton, inherited box seats, and an easy disregard for all that. By going straight to the disregard I'd hoped to imply the rest. I had also meant to wipe out any trace of the public school virtues—sharpness of dress, keenness of manner, spanking cleanliness, freshness, niceness, sincerity—I used to cultivate.

By now I'd been absorbed so far into my performance that nothing else came naturally. But I never quite forgot that I was performing. In the first couple of years there'd been some spirit of play in creating the part, refining it, watching it pass. There'd been pleasure in implying a personal history through purely dramatic effects of manner and speech without ever committing an expository lie, and pleasure in doubleness itself: there was more to me than people knew!

All that was gone. When I caught myself in the act now I felt embarrassed. It seemed a stale, conventional role, and four years of it had left me a stranger even to those I called my friends.

I wanted out. That was partly why I'd chosen Columbia. I liked how the city seethed up against the school, mocking its theoretical seclusion with hustle and noise, the din of people going and getting and making. Things that mattered at Princeton or Yale couldn't possibly withstand this battering of raw, unironic life. You didn't go to eating clubs at Columbia, you went to jazz clubs. You had a girlfriend—no, a lover—with psychiatric problems, and friends with foreign accents. You read newspapers on the subway and looked at tourists with a cool, anthropological gaze. You said *crosstown express*. You said *the Village*. You ate weird food. No other boy in my class would be going there.

It wasn't exactly true that I'd told no expository lies. Most of my stories had been meant to seem autobiographical, and thus to give a false picture of my family and my life at home—of who I was. I'd allowed myself to do this by thinking that, after all, they were just stories. But they weren't really stories, not like "Big Two-Hearted River" was a story, or "Soldier's Home." It struck me that Hemingway's willingness to let himself be seen as he was, in uncertainty or meanness or fear, even empty of feeling, somehow gave the charge of truth to everything else. My stories were designed to make me appear as I was not. They were props in an act. I couldn't read any of them without thrusting the pages away in mortification.

I couldn't write like that again, but didn't know how else to write—how to go about making something that was true. I was frozen. For the simple relief of putting words on paper I continued to type out Hemingway's stories, slowly, meditatively, a page or so a day. I had the hope that something here would send me off on a story of my own. No luck so far, but I kept at it, page after page.

Krebs acquired the nausea in regard to experience that is the result of untruth or exaggeration. . . . In this way he lost everything.

I knew just how Krebs felt.

Everybody else was writing up a storm. As one of the top scholars in our class, Bill had been awarded a private study in the basement of the library. He worked there, so I didn't see much of him, but when I did he was thoughtful and tense. I had trouble getting a smile out of him; if I succeeded I felt a gratitude I found myself resenting. He told me he had a story in the works, and that was all he'd admit to. The un-boyish sadness I'd seen in Bill that winter had darkened. He seemed lost in the contemplation of something doleful, even tragic, that I could only suppose was finding its way into his new work.

Purcell had a story going as well. With not entirely charming matter-of-factness he told me it was the best thing he'd ever written, and professed to be astonished at the ease of its writing. I didn't see any mystery here: if he kept cutting chapel he'd never have to expose his story to judgment, and it was at least partly the prospect of judgment that had me all in knots.

George Kellogg decided to submit a new version of a story we'd run in *Troubadour* that winter, an account of a man bullying his wife at the dinner table while their son eats his veal cutlet and doesn't say a word. No boy had ever won two audiences. There wasn't any rule against it, but I thought it was pretty damned piggish of George to try to snag Hemingway after landing Frost. Just knowing he was in the race became a vexation, and it got worse when I went to his room to ask about the manuscripts for the next issue of the review. George hadn't been passing them around.

He answered when I knocked, though for once his good manners deserted him and he kept typing away on his massive old black Underwood while I stood just inside the door. The machine looked as big as an organ. It made a deep, emphatic, methodical sound. The blinds were drawn, the windows closed, and the air felt swampy. I could hear the muffled plock of a tennis ball somewhere outside. Finally George stopped, but remained hunched over the keys.

I asked him about the manuscripts.

Oh, *them*, he said. They're over there. He jerked his head at a stack of papers on his dresser. Take 'em.

Have you read them yet?

What? I don't know. A few. A couple. He kept his back to me as I crossed the room and picked up the manuscripts.

I hear you're working on that last *Troubadour* story.

That's all of them, he said. Okay?

When I closed the door he started typing again.

All through my dorm I heard typewriters. Maybe it was nothing new, maybe I'd just lost my filter, the way every voice around you will suddenly flood into your head, each with its own rhythm and tone. One machine went off in high crackling bursts like strings of cheap firecrackers. Another, even lower than George's, grumbled and surged like the engines of a ship. I tried not to listen for them.

With our editor playing the possessed artist, I had to play the burgher—had to act like the director of publication whose title I bore—and make sure *Troubadour* got to the printer in time. The deadline for presenting our last issue to Mr. Rice, the faculty adviser, was just days away, the same Monday our Hemingway stories were due. I gave myself up to reading submissions and forcing them on my fellow editors, and tried not to listen to other boys' typewriters, and typed nothing myself.

We scheduled the final editorial meeting for Sunday night. I'd lobbied for Friday but got voted down because Miss Cobb's graduating class was joining ours that night for the traditional Farewell Assembly. These assemblies were said to be Neronic in their carnality, like the fabled last night of an ocean crossing, and none of us questioned the truth of the stories we'd heard. Since the girls weren't going to see us again and we weren't going to see them again, why be coy? Our regular dances were licentious enough, within the limits set by the vigilant, and of course envious, spinsters who rode shotgun at these affairs. But it was a truth repeated by all of us, and made ever truer by repetition, that at the Farewell Assembly no amount of jealous virginal watchdogging would prove equal to the girls' desire to be alone with us in broom closets and steam tunnels.

Nobody wanted to miss out. I didn't either, especially after I got a letter from Rain. This took me by surprise. We'd had our brief grapple at the Halloween dance, but I hadn't seen her since she tried to make off with my *Fountainhead* on the train, and she'd certainly never sent me a letter before. It was a perfumed, chatty little piece with no purpose except the unstated but obvious one of nailing down a partner for the Assembly. She must've figured she could do worse than me, and probably would do worse if she left it to chance, as the desirables of each school had already begun pairing off through just such letters as this. I had not forgotten how it felt to dance with Rain, how she returned the pressure of my thighs and played her fingers over the back of my neck. And the then-painful fact that she had immediately taken up with another boy (Jack Broome of sacred memory!) after being pried away from me, the sheer impersonality of her ardor, snuffed any scruples I might've felt and gave the lurid tint of revenge to my anticipations.

Yet I had tried to set the editorial meeting for that night. Time was running out, and I wanted to put *Troubadour* to bed so I'd have the weekend to finish the story I hadn't even begun. There were other Rains in the world, but only one Ernest Hemingway.

And there was another reason I had tried for Friday night. Saturday was Purcell's day of reckoning. If he didn't show up for chapel that afternoon, he'd be long gone after dinner, when we gathered to make our picks. I wanted him there, I needed him to help me sort through this pile of submissions in which only two poems and one story stood out as clear choices. Purcell was brutal in his judgments but he was also shrewd, and finally willing to allow that he despised this or that manuscript rather less than the rest.

The other two would be no help at all, George in favor of everything and Bill cryptic and elusive. *There are a lot of cats in this story*, he'd say, or *I didn't know it rained that hard in Athens*, then shrug and fall silent. Though never overtly so, his responses were much more destructive than Purcell's. They left you feeling dazed, flatfooted. It was exactly the way he played squash—never slamming the ball head-on, like I did, but breezily tapping it through some sly angle so it died in the corner.

On Friday Big Jeff made it known that if his cousin got kicked out for cutting next afternoon's chapel, he was leaving with him. I heard this at lunch and wouldn't have believed it except that our table master refused to contradict it. It made no sense. Big Jeff loved the school—anybody could see that. He was an odd duck, and in a place less sure of itself and therefore harder on its eccentrics he would've had some rough sledding. Here he received the protections of a holy fool, and he sensed these indulgences if not their reason, and basked in them. It was already plain that he would become one of those alums who return constantly to the Alma Mater, and fatten her with bon-bons from his swelling portfolio, and one day leave her so much of what his own children have been anticipating, and even bud-geting into their current expenses, that the disappointed heirs seriously consider paupering themselves further in attempts to break a will that the Old Boys' office would already have bound in legal iron.

So why would Big Jeff let his cousin's obstinacy and pride come between him and the school he loved? He certainly couldn't help Purcell by threatening to leave—that was ridiculous. The school was no less hostage to its rules than we were, and he knew it.

Why, then? Love. *Worship*. This was a curious and agree-able twist, Big Jeff spanieling after his cousin with his tongue out, barking at phantoms as he followed him into martyrdom. It somehow put the whole thing in a farcical light, as Purcell must have understood, because he was furious. First he collared Big Jeff in Blaine Hall after lunch and made some kind of scene. I wasn't there, but word got around. Then, that afternoon, he came to Big Jeff's room, just down from mine, and gave him another brow-beating. *This has nothing to do with you! You have no right! No right!*

I listened to Purcell yell and Big Jeff murmur indiscernibly in reply, then the door slammed and I went back to my story. So far I'd been unable to complete even a paragraph without yanking the paper out of the machine.

I was still at my post when the bell rang for dinner, and when everyone came back from dinner. All up and down the hall I heard my classmates preparing for the Farewell Assembly, roaring in the showers, going from room to room to be admired in their tuxes under the pretext of having a tie adjusted, a cummerbund cinched tight. Strange how our voices deepened and slowed when we dressed up like this. It was a kind of hysteria that made us not giddy but deliberate. The air was festively steamy from everyone showering, and smelled of Old Spice.

My tux, delivered with the others that morning, hung in the closet with a stiff pleated shirt of brilliant whiteness. I laid them out on my bed with the patent leather shoes, then went back to my desk. All I needed was a good beginning, something to give me a start in the morning.

The hall grew quiet as the others left. I watched them cross the quad in a long dark line. In the ashen dusk, their shirt collars seemed to float like lights on a hazy sea. Their deep voices still reached me from the far side of the quad, carried on a breeze that smelled of mown grass and rustled in the creeper outside my window, and later brought me the sounds of Lester Lanin's orchestra and the laughter of girls.

All this was a distraction at first, then faded behind a waking dream. Hemingway had chosen my story and taken a shine to me and hired me to work on the *Pilar*. We were cruising one after-noon with his wife, Mary, and a couple of their friends. The friendship seemed unaccountable. The woman was catty and the man treated the crew rudely and boasted of his skill at fishing, all of which Hemingway endured patiently though not without giving me a resigned look as I served yet another round of drinks. Finally the man's wife told him to *please* go catch himself a fish and shut the hell *up* about it. He could catch a fish here, couldn't he, Ernest? They *were* in the middle of the goddamned ocean, weren't they? Hemingway allowed that in fact they were in very good fishing grounds. You would have to be cursed, he said, not to catch a fish here.

The man demurred. He was particular about his gear and hadn't thought to bring it along today. When his wife said he could surely use Ernest's, the man said he wouldn't hear of it, thanks anyway.

Now darling, don't be such a *stick*, his wife said.

So he was buckled into the hot seat with a pole in his hands and sure enough he had a strike within the first few minutes. The pole bent and the line sang out. Oh Jesus, the man said, then grunted as the pole somehow jumped its holster and yanked him forward. A great marlin leaped high off the port side, shook itself, crashed back into the water. I'm sick, the man said, I'm going to be sick.

Take the pole! Hemingway told me, then helped the man out of the seat and strapped me in. I played the fish while the man puked over the side of the boat. He refused all invitations to return to the chair, so I worked the big fellow for a couple of hours while Hemingway stood behind me and offered counsel now and then but mostly left the job to me. Once the marlin was played out Mary took the pole to reel him alongside while Hemingway and I waited to set the grapple hook and winch him up.

This is an unhappy case, Hemingway said. He is a good man who married badly and should not drink. He was very brave in the war.

We pulled up to the dock at sunset. A bunch of gawkers came over. That's some kind of monster you've got there, one of them said. Who hooked him?

He did, I said, and nodded at the man.

Hemingway stood beside me. You have done well today, he said. You have done very well today.

When Bill White came back from the library at midnight I still hadn't written a word. Didn't you go to the dance? he said.

I was working.

Bill sat on his bed and slowly unlaced his shoes. He fell back and stared up at the ceiling. You could still go, he said.

No point. They'll be shutting down pretty soon.

Working on your story?

Working on my story. You?

Yeah, sure. Bill rolled onto his side and watched as I pulled the empty page from my typewriter and slipped it into my desk drawer, under the full pages I'd copied from "Soldier's Home." He said, I saw George coming back from the dance.

George went? No kidding. I've never seen him in a tux. How'd he look?

Was he in a tux? I suppose he must've been. I didn't really notice.

Can't blame you, I said, then added—meanly, helplessly— George makes everything look like tweed.

Bill didn't answer.

I guess he finished his story, I said.

I guess so, Bill said. How's yours going?

He said this in a worn, tender way that surprised me. We were almost at the end of our years together, and without ever fighting or deviling each other as most other roommates did, we were farther from being friends than on our first day. We had made ourselves unknowable behind our airs and sardonic courtesies, and the one important truth I'd discovered about him we'd silently agreed never to acknowledge. Many such agreements had evolved between us. No acknowledgment of who we really were—of trouble, weakness, or doubt—of our worries about the life ahead and the sort of men we were becoming. Never; not a word. We'd kept everything witty and cool, until the air between us was so ironized that to say anything in earnest would have been a breach of manners, even of trust.

But as young boys here we had marked each other for friendship. I still felt the possibility, and it troubled me that we had always let it slip. Mostly I blamed Bill, for not coming out from behind his polish. He'd been in the dumps for weeks yet he wouldn't break cover and talk straight to me, though we surely had things to talk about, more than he knew. The sadder he got, the more remote. Until now.

How's yours going?

His question was serious, the interest behind it wearily intimate, undefended, as if he had lost whatever push it took to support his urbanity. I was so wrung out myself, so tired of all this beggarly waiting for words, that I actually felt tempted to tell him the truth—that I hadn't written anything, and couldn't. Poised right on the brink, I still held back, perhaps sensing that the moment it started, once I allowed myself the comfort of his interest, I wouldn't be able to stop; that the relief of confessing this paralysis might betray me into other confessions. In some murky way I recognized my own impatience to tear off the mask, and it spooked me.

Lester Lanin's orchestra was playing "Auld Lang Syne." A few voices sang raggedly along, boys and girls together.

It's going fine, I said. Like gangbusters. Yours?

Oh . . . same here. Like a house afire. Like crazy. Like nobody's business.

When Purcell showed up for chapel on Saturday afternoon he took his place on the steps and waited in line for the processional to begin, eyes dead ahead, the fierce helpless blush on his pale, freckled neck his only response to the looks he was drawing from the younger boys and the studious inattention of the older. But as the organ sounded the first notes he raised his voice with the rest of us—*For all the saints, who from their labors rest*—and marched up the aisle to his seat in the second row without letting the words trail off as most of us did. He sang every verse and then sat straight and intent through the chaplain's readings and remarks, and when we were left in silence he bowed his head and did not stir.

At the end of the service the headmaster got up to congratulate the sixth-form dance committee on a successful Assembly, and we all applauded, and then kept on, decorously but persistently, beyond any conceivable gratitude to the dance committee, and Purcell must have known it was for him—in celebration that he was still with us, and in tribute to his selflessness in yielding dear principle for his cousin's sake. Though he was clapping too and looking up at the headmaster, his neck had again turned scarlet.

I had my own idea about his change of heart; that it had less to do with sparing Big Jeff a painful separation from the school than with sparing himself the absurd, humiliating spectacle of Big Jeff throwing himself on Purcell's very own funeral pyre. But I applauded him with the rest, for the dignity of his surrender; no winking or mugging, no holding back, no hamming it up to signal derisory assent. He had something, Purcell. Sand. Backbone. *Class*, I guess you could say.

At the editorial meeting that night we made our decisions without serious disagreement until we came to the last manuscript, a story by a classmate named Buckles who'd been submitting work all year to no effect. This story did not seem to me any better than the ones we'd rejected, and I said so.

What's it *about?* George said. I can't even tell what it's *about.* He said this with such violence that Purcell and Bill and I were made shy for a moment. George usually took his post at the editor's desk, but tonight he was sitting by the door, cross and itchy.

Still, this is his last shot, Bill said. Graduation issue.

That's true, Purcell said. It's now or never for Buckles.

The story's not *that* bad, Bill said.

It's not that good, I said.

Bulldog Buckles, Bill said. Never say die. Remember that story about Geronimo?

We laughed, all but George. "The Forked Tongue," he said sullenly.

What? Purcell said.

It was called "The Forked Tongue." Let me see this one again.

We watched George glance over the first page. Just listen to this, he said. He read a few lines aloud.

That's not so bad, Purcell said.

There's something there, Bill said.

Come on, I said.

Oh for Christ's sake, run the stupid thing! George said. Who cares? It's not like the rest of this crap's about to set the world on fire. When we looked at him he bristled and said, Well? Is it?

Of course the answer was no. Our schoolboy journal was not going to set the world on fire. But for the past year we'd been acting on the faith that it might, choosing and shaping every issue with the solemnity of Big Jeff designing a spaceship. So, the game was over—that's what George was telling us, the prick, the spoiler. He'd somehow lost his innocence and now he couldn't rest until we too had seen that our sanctum sanctorum was only a storage room, our high purposes not worth a fart in a gale of wind.

But George, of all people—what had worked this change in him? What had he been writing up in that airless room, what vein of acid knowledge had he struck?

Okay, I said. What the hell. Let's run it.

So we'd come to the end; our last issue laid to rest, albeit with a bullet in its head. The others fled the room, leaving me to order and stack the manuscripts and hand them off to the incoming editor, a fifth former who'd been sitting in on the meeting to see how it was done. He looked pretty disappointed.

Mr. Rice'll need those first thing tomorrow, I told him.

I know.

It was late, past midnight, but I was too jumpy to make another start at the story that was due later that morning, so I figured I'd warm up with a few rejection notes. Usually George took care of that but he had apparently abandoned his duties.

The office machine was a tinny portable that jumped a little every time you struck a key. I wrote three or four letters and took a break. It was tomb-quiet in there, the walls soundproofed by bookcases crammed with student lit mags, the overflow stacked in precarious towers on the two file cabinets and the editor's desk. Here were the *Troubadours* of Andover, Milton, Dobbs Ferry, Taft, St. Timothy's and St. Paul's and St. Mark's, Nottingham, Hill, Woodberry Forest, Madeira, Portsmouth Priory, Foxcroft, Kent, Emma Willard, Culver, Thacher, Roxbury Latin, Baldwin and Lawrenceville, Miss Cobb's and Miss Fine's and Miss Porter's, Peddie, Hotchkiss, Pomfret, Choate, on and on and on . . .

As director of publication I sometimes came here to file the new arrivals, though mostly I just sat at George's desk and gloated at being in the middle of all this writing. But what sort of writing was it, really? I took down a review from Andover and flipped through the stories, then looked at one from Deerfield and another from Hill. Within a few sentences every story seemed familiar, the same stuff we ran—mannered experiment, disillusioned portrait of family or school, all designed to show what a superior person the writer was.

Were the girls any better? I picked up a copy of *Cantiamo*, the review from Miss Cobb's; it was a back issue, five years old. The first story concerned the superficiality of a woman prepping her house for a bridge party. I skipped to the next, called "Summer Dance," and the smirk this title provoked died on my lips after the first line.

I hope nobody saw me pick up the cigarette butt off the sidewalk, but I'm all out and getting shaky and it's a nice long one, with just a smudge of lipstick from the old bird who dropped it when her bus pulled up.

I kept reading. The narrator is at a bus stop, heading home after a typing class at the Y. She smokes the butt while she waits, even when it becomes apparent that another girl has caught her in the act and is completely grossed out. *I don't really care*, the narrator says, *because I don't know her. If I knew her, or if she was a boy, that would be different.* As she smokes she thinks up a lie to scare up some cigarette money from her mother; another fee for supplies in the typing class.

She rides the bus across the city—Columbus—and walks home through a neighborhood of brick apartment buildings. Her mother's apartment is on the third floor. It's sweltering inside. The narrator's little sister is watching TV, her mother's in her bedroom with a headache. She calls out to the narrator—Ruth, it turns out her name is—and Ruth puts some ice in a dishtowel and carries it into the darkened room. She sits on the edge of the bed, holding the icepack to her mother's forehead, and after making some tender inquiries slips in the lie about the typing supplies. Her mother sighs and says, *Okay, of course, take what you need.* She tells Ruth that two of her friends called, but asks her please not to make any plans as she feels really awful and needs help with Naomi.

Ruth goes into the kitchen and looks at the notepad by the phone. The first message is from a girl she grew up with. It's the second time she's called since Ruth got home for the summer and though Ruth feels guilty for not calling her back she knows she won't do it this time either. The other message is from Caroline Fallon, a classmate at the boarding school Ruth attends on scholarship. She dials the number immediately.

The two girls make clever talk about how bored they are. Ruth calls her mother *Maman*, and describes her indisposition in terms that make Caroline laugh. Then Caroline asks if she'd like to go to a dance at the country club that night. When Ruth hesitates, she apologizes for the late notice and says, by way of explanation, *They need girls.*

Okay, Ruth says. *I need boys.*

There's just one thing, Caroline says. *It's so ridiculous, but anyway—can I give your name as Lewis instead of Levine?*

Lewis?

You know, Lewis, Logan, something like that. I'm sorry, Ruthie. Club rules.

I see.

It's disgusting. I probably shouldn't have called you.

No, that's all right. That's fine. Tell them Windsor.

Windsor! You are a stitch! I mean, Ruthie Windsor!

Ruth Anne Windsor.

Ruth and her mother argue over her plans for the night, and Ruth handles it so deftly that her mother gets out of bed to coax her back from desolation and take in the waist of a smart old evening gown of her own that Ruth's been coveting. When she leaves the apartment she has to stop and catch her breath, she's so heady with the relief of escape, *like getting out of granny's hospital room.*

Then the dance—the convertibles in the parking lot, the Japanese lanterns along the path to the ballroom, the music, the boys. Ruth sees that the boys have noticed her, but the one who catches her notice happens also to be the boy Caroline has in her sights. His name is Colson. He and his friend Gary sit down at Ruth and Caroline's table. They're both handsome, but Gary's sort of bland and Colson's broody and smart—too smart really for Caroline—and just as Ruth feels his interest shift toward her she senses a growing restlessness in Caroline, a watchful formless unease. Something's wrong and Caroline doesn't yet know what it is, but she'll know soon enough if things follow their present course, and she will hate Ruth for it and drop her like a toad.

Normally that wouldn't bother her. Ruth likes to compete with other girls, and she fancies this Colson with his rumbly voice and hooded eyes. At any other time she would encourage his attentions.

But this isn't any other time. She's at the beginning of a long summer. One of the convertibles in the parking lot belongs to Caroline, and already Ruth has gotten used to being rescued from her hot apartment for breezy drives to movie theaters and the pool at Caroline's house. This is only the first of many dances at the club, and she wants to be invited to the rest. Caroline won't just drop her if she feels betrayed, she will make sure Colson knows that Ruth is here tonight under false pretenses, and exactly what those pretenses are. How interested will he be then?

Lousy odds, Ruth thinks. She fastens her attention on Gary. He warms to it, and Colson withdraws moodily before resuming his languid banter with Caroline, who comes brightly to life. But Ruth is still aware of Colson and knows that he's aware of her. Something may yet come of it before this summer is over, something secret where Ruth can get her own back. Even now the current between them is so obvious to her that she can hardly believe Caroline doesn't feel it. Ruth stands and takes Gary's hand to lead him toward the dance floor. Caroline smiles up at Ruth and lifts her glass. *Good—she doesn't know. Everything's okay.*

Everything's okay. That was the last line in the story, this story where nothing was okay. I went back to the beginning and read it again, slowly this time, feeling all the while as if my inmost vault had been smashed open and looted and every hidden thing spread out across these pages. From the very first sentence I was looking myself right in the face.

It went beyond the obvious parallels. Where I really recognized myself was in the momentary, undramatic details of Ruth's life and habits of thought. The typing class, say. What could be more ordinary than spending your summer days in a typing class at the Y? That was exactly what I'd done for part of the previous summer, yet I'd never once mentioned it to my schoolmates just *because* it was so completely ordinary, and uncool. And taking a bus to get there! No character in my stories ever rode a bus.

The whole thing came straight from the truthful diary I'd never kept: the typing class, the bus, the apartment; all mine. And mine too the calculations and stratagems, the throwing-over of old friends for new, the shameless manipulation of a needy, loving parent and the desperation to flee not only the need but the love itself. Then the sweetness of flight, the lightness and joy of escape. And, yes, the almost physical attraction to privilege, the resolve to be near it at any cost: sycophancy, lies, self-suppression, the masking of ambitions and desires, the slow cowardly burn of resentment toward those for whose favor you have falsified yourself. Every moment of it was true.

How do you begin to write truly? I went back to that first sentence. *I hope nobody saw me pick up the cigarette butt off the sidewalk . . .* It made me cringe. This was not how I would ever want to be seen, though in my own cigarette-craving I had done that very thing, and more than once.

What the hell—let's see how it felt to write it. I rolled a fresh sheet into the typewriter and started pecking it out: *I hope nobody saw me . . .* Then the keys jammed. I separated them and they jammed again. That sentence did not want to be written, but I wrote it still. And there I was, winner of the Cassidy English Prize, future protégé of Lionel Trilling, bending to the sidewalk for a lipsticked butt.

I had stopped going to confession right after my mother died. Even as a young boy I'd performed it grudgingly and with no payoff I was ever aware of. But in writing those words I felt at least an intuition of gracious release. To strip yourself of pretense is to overthrow a hard master, the fear of giving yourself away, and in that one sentence I gave myself away beyond all recall. Now there was nothing to do but go on.

Word by word I gave it all away. I changed Ruth's first name to mine, in order to place myself unmistakably in the frame of these acts and designs, but kept Levine, because it made unmistakable what my own last name did not. I changed the city to Seattle, Caroline to James, and brought other particulars into line. I didn't have a lot of adjusting to do. These thoughts were my thoughts, this life my own.

It took a long time. The typewriter kept inching back, and as it retreated I leaned farther and farther over the desk until the discomfort broke my trance. Then I'd have to return the machine to the starting line and get up and pace the room a while to ease my back before bending once again to the work.

I finished the story just before the bell rang for breakfast. I read it through and fixed a few typos, but otherwise it needed no correction. It was done. Anyone who read this story would know who I was.

WHEN IN
DISGRACE
WITH FORTUNE

As I left the dining hall one morning Mr. Ramsey took my elbow and asked if he might have a word with me. He guided me in the direction of the headmaster's garden, away from the stream of boys going to their rooms or their chores. He kept his hold on me as we walked, in what I took to be a confidential English way, so I bowed my head and looked grave. It puzzled me to be singled out like this. Though I had done well in Mr. Ramsey's class the year before, I'd kept my distance and so had he.

You've not wasted your time here, he said.

I knew that Mr. Ramsey had been on the Cassidy Prize committee, so I thought he was referring to my Shakespeare essay; but when I thanked him he looked annoyed and waved it off.

We're not here to talk about essays, he said. One can imagine a world without essays. It would be a little poorer, of course, like a world without . . . chess, but one could live in it. Mr. Ramsey let go of my elbow and stopped beside the low stone wall that ran around the garden. A skinny black squirrel with tufted ears scrambled up the wall and began chattering at us.

Stories, though—one could not live in a world without stories.

No. No, sir.

Without stories one would hardly know what world one was *in*. But I'm not saying this very well. Mr. Ramsey stared out over the garden. It has to do with self-consciousness, he said. Though I'm no believer, I find it interesting that self-consciousness is associated with the Fall. Nakedness and shame. Knowledge of ourselves as a thing apart, and bound to die. *Exile*. We speak of self-consciousness as a burden or a problem, and so it is—the problem being how to use it to bring ourselves *out* of exile. Whereas our tendency is to lose ourselves in the distance, wouldn't you say?

The squirrel approached to within a foot of us and reared up, obviously expecting a handout. Someone had been sneaking him scraps, probably a younger boy, homesick, missing his dog.

That squirrel looks about ready to take us down, I said.

Lost in the distance, Mr. Ramsey said again. It's a wonder we're not all barking. And of course we would be if we hadn't any way to use self-consciousness against itself, or rather against its worst inclinations—morbidity, narcissism, paranoia, grandiosity, that lot. We have *somehow* to turn a profit on it. Which is, I must say, exactly what that story of yours does. "Summer Dance." A marvelous story! Pure magic. No—no—not magic. *Alchemy*. The dross of self-consciousness transformed into the gold of self-knowledge. Enough. I see I'm embarrassing you. But I had to tell you, for my own sake if not yours, what a superior piece of writing that is.

I thanked Mr. Ramsey for his kind words and asked how he'd happened to read my story. I had dropped my only copy in the submission box, from which I assumed it had been forwarded to Idaho with the others.

I chose the final entries, he said. Seeing my surprise, he said, Really, now, you didn't suppose we sent Mr. Ernest Hemingway every story you fellows came up with, *did* you? All thirty-four of them? Oh no. I skimmed off the three best and sent him those, though I knew it was strictly pro forma after I'd read the first page of "Summer Dance." And I was right, wasn't I?

Sir?

Ernest Hemingway chose your story. Hadn't any choice, really. I'm no believer, as I say, but I do believe in the existence of what one can only call gifts—gifts without a giver, if you will, but gifts all the same. That which cannot be earned or deserved. Rewards for nothing. A scandal to the virtuous and hardworking, but there you are. I'll admit to some envy here.

Ernest Hemingway chose my story?

We're asking you not to say anything until it's announced in the school paper tomorrow. Didn't want to spring it on you all at once like that—out of the blue. Wanted to give you a chance to draw breath, and of course add a personal note of congratulations. Your story will run with my interview.

I was glad for the day of grace I'd been given. After my last class that afternoon I went AWOL across the river and mucked through freshly ploughed fields to the tallest of the neighboring hills, Mount Winston as we called it. Mount Winston had been a smoker's roost when I served with that band of incorrigibles; to judge from all the butts moldering up here in the dimples and clefts of exposed shale, it still was.

I paced the hilltop, exhausted but too nervous to sit. In my classes the blood-roar in my head had rendered me nearly deaf. Most of this was explosive relief and exhilaration, yet with a thumping underpulse of dread. It was one thing to confide your hidden life to a piece of paper in an empty room, quite another to have it broadcast.

A warm wind blew across the hilltop, and with it the faint

cries of boys chasing balls. The school lawns and fields were a rich, unreal green against the muddy brown expanse of surrounding farmland. Between the wooded banks of the river two shells raced upstream, oars flashing. The chapel with its tall crenellated bell tower and streaming pennant looked like an engraving in a child's book. From this height it was possible to see into the dream that produced the school, not mere English-envy but the yearning for a chivalric world apart from the din of scandal and cheap dispute, the hustles and schemes of modernity itself. As I recognized this dream I also sensed its futility, but so what? I loved my school no less for being gallantly unequal to our appetites—more, if anything. With still a month to graduation I was already damp with nostalgia. I stretched out on a slab of rock. The sun in my face and radiant warmth on my back lulled me to sleep. Then the wind cooled and I woke with a wolfish hunger and started back.

The school newspaper came out twice a month. They left it in the foyer of the dining hall so we could pick it up going into breakfast, and on these mornings we were allowed to read at the table—our faces obscured by the open wings of the plainly named *News*, or bent over pages folded neatly beside high-piled plates, which most boys, perhaps from long study of their commuting fathers, could empty without a glance. The thought of sitting there while everyone read my story gave me the creeps, but I had to go. I had to see what Ernest Hemingway thought of my work.

The kitchen sounds and chink of crockery gave depth to the quiet of the hall. Boys glanced up from their papers to sneak looks in my direction. I couldn't eat, but I poured myself a cup of coffee and spread the front page over my empty plate. The opening of "Summer Dance" ran down three columns on the left, to be continued inside; the fourth and last column contained the telephone interview with Hemingway, surmounted by our art master's caricature. Mr. Ramsey had left out his own questions, so Hemingway seemed to be speaking in monologue.

You can tell your boy there that this is pretty good work. Pretty damned good work, considering. He knows what he's writing about, more than he's telling, and that's good. That's always good. He is writing cleanly and well about what he knows and he's writing from his conscience and that always raises the stakes. This is the story of a conscience and that kind of story if it's honest always has something for another conscience to learn from, even an old wreck like mine. These are true human beings here, I mean true on the page, though I'm guessing they are true in other ways. If they are, they will never forgive him. This I can promise. If your boy had asked me, I would have told him to wait till they were all dead.

Am I kidding? Sure. Sure I am. The stories you have to write will always make someone hate your guts. If they don't you're just producing words.

Advice . . . Don't take advice, I never did. And don't get swellheaded. Writers are just like everyone else, only worse. Did he rewrite the story forty times? He could throw away some stuff, I've thrown away enough in my time. The kid knows what he's writing about and that's good, now he should go out and know some other things to write about.

But I don't mean wars, not the way you probably think I mean. You don't go to war as a tourist. War'll get you killed and dead men don't write books. Same with hunting. Same with the sauce. Take Joyce. A rummy. Chained to his desk. Liked to read his work out loud, pretty tenor voice. Blind as a bat. You know what his wife told me? Said he ought to go lion hunting, that it would be good for his work and I should take him lion hunting. Can you imagine that? James Joyce lion hunting, with those eyes? Maybe I should have, come to think of it.

Watch the sauce. The sauce kills more writers than war, just takes longer. If you're going up against the giant killer you'd better be damned sure you can win. Some of us can, some can't. Scott never had a chance, poor soft [———]. Mouth like a girl's. Between the rum and that pretty mouth and that wife of his he never had a chance. But he didn't write drunk, not like Bill Faulkner. With Bill Faulkner you can tell, right in the middle of a sentence, where the mash kicked in. Called me a coward once. A coward. I had to have Buck Lanham set him straight.

Watch the sauce. And don't pay any attention to what the [———] say about you. They've said everything about me. What the hell. They'll die and then they'll be dead.

What else? Don't talk about your writing. If you talk about your writing you will touch something you shouldn't touch and it will fall apart and you will have nothing. Get up at first light and work like hell. Let your wife sleep in, it'll pay off later. Watch your blood pressure. Read. Read James Joyce and Bill Faulkner and Isak Dinesen, that beautiful writer. Read Scott Fitzgerald. Hold on to your friends. Work like hell and make enough money to go someplace else, some other country where the [———] Feds can't get at you.

Did I say keep your friends? Keep your friends, hold on to your friends. Don't lose your friends.

I don't know. I guess that's it. That's the sermon for today.

In another week I would meet Ernest Hemingway, and walk alone with him in the headmaster's garden. He had chosen my story and made special mention of it for everyone to read. There was no excuse for me to feel anything but joy. I knew this, sure, but what did his blood pressure or James Joyce's wife or Fitzgerald's pretty mouth or sleeping late or getting up early have to do with my story? I didn't want Ernest Hemingway's advice, I wanted his attention.

True, he said I was doing pretty damned good work, but his *considering* sort of canceled that out. The part where he said I knew what I wrote about, that was good, that was true—so why did he have to spoil it with that business about knowing something else? Did *this* story need me to know something else? And what, exactly, should I have thrown away? An example would've been nice, if he could actually find one.

The best part was about "Summer Dance" being a story of conscience, giving other consciences something to learn from. But why not take the obvious next step and mention the courage this kind of story required? He knew, he had to know from writing "Soldier's Home" and "The End of Something" how it felt to expose yourself like this for the sake of a story, to make it living and true. Why didn't he say so?

The answer came to me as I studied the shape of the interview. Hemingway had begun by talking about my story and surely would've gone on talking about it if he hadn't been derailed into all this trivia by Mr. Ramsey's questions, now cleverly removed to make Hemingway sound like a maundering, self-important old bore with his beard in a drink. It was an injustice both to him and to me, and I resented it, as I resented the prissy editing of the interview. I had a vision of Mr. Ramsey, *Lolita's* Paladin, sworn enemy of censors everywhere, hunched over the typescript like some lip-reading Soviet goon as he cut the guts out of Ernest Hemingway's language.

Hemingway had been ill-served and so had I. But he'd be here soon, and free to talk about my story without interruption. I could wait.

A hand gripped my shoulder. It was Mr. Rice. Looking thoughtfully down at me, he squeezed until it almost hurt, then he gave a little nod and let go. Well done, sir, he said. A commendable effusion. And because your Mr. Hemingway had the sense to recognize it, I will try—I will *try*—to forgive his boorish traducement of his betters. But I must warn you I shall probably fail.

Nice job, a boy across the table said.

Yeah, it's okay, another boy said. I read the whole thing.

George Kellogg fell in with me on my way to class. At first he said nothing. We walked together, hands in our pockets, shoes scuffing on the brick walkway. I'm disappointed, naturally, he said. But I'm glad for you, for writing that story. To tell the truth, if I hadn't seen your name on it I wouldn't have thought it was yours. Which goes to show what a big step you took. It's a good story, a really good story, and you should be proud of it.

I thanked him and said I'd like to read his sometime.

No you wouldn't.

Oh, come on.

No, he said, and that was all.

With only weeks to go until graduation, my class was drawing close. You could see the change—our studied nonchalance cracking and falling away like the shell of an egg. Even boys who had lived almost in exile, either by their choice or ours, were led inward by the tribal feeling that had come upon us. This was both urgent and ordinary. We had seen it happen to other classes, and been told that it would happen to ours with such tedious frequency that we became knowing and wary; but despite our knowingness, it happened anyway. I didn't want to lose my place in the circle, so of course I was afraid of what my schoolmates would think after reading "Summer Dance."

My fears came to nothing. Masters and boys alike told me pretty much what George had said—with plain goodwill and something else, something like relief, as if they'd felt all along that I was holding back, and could breathe easier now that I'd spoken up.

A manila envelope was leaning against the door of my room. I hefted it—a book—and carried it inside. A note scrawled on the envelope said: *You should have this. P.*

I opened the envelope and slid the book out. It was a first edition of *In Our Time*. I sank to the edge of my bed and sat there studying the cover. Bill came through the door not long after. He took in the book at a glance and said, Purcell?

I nodded.

To the victor go the spoils. Here, he said, and took his Waterman fountain pen from his pocket and tossed it on my bed.

Bill, what're you doing? I can't take that.

Oh, I think you can. What's mine is yours, right? Bill went to his desk, opened the drawer, rummaged for something, then slammed it shut and stood facing out the window. He was leaning on the desktop with both hands as if trying to push it through the floor.

I'm sorry he didn't pick your story, I said. I'm glad he chose mine but I'm sorry he didn't choose yours.

Is that all you can think about? Ernest fucking Hemingway? He couldn't have *chosen* mine. I never handed one in.

Why not?

None of your business. He turned and looked at me. Have you ever been inside a synagogue?

No. Well, once. On a field trip.

That's not what I mean.

Then no.

You're Catholic, aren't you?

Not exactly.

You used to go into town with the Catholic boys.

For a while. Not anymore, not since fourth form.

So you're a *lapsed* Catholic. The point is you were raised Catholic.

Yes.

So it's fair to say you haven't had the experience of doing what this person in your story does.

What's that?

You know. You *know*.

That's not exactly true.

Don't give me that shit. Okay, so you've taken an interest in this person's situation. So you've *imagined* what it's like. Bully for you. That doesn't make it your situation. It isn't your situation, and it isn't your story. That was *my* story, you fucking leech. That was my story and you know it.

I'd been all set to explain myself, right up to the moment he called me a leech, but now I just shrugged and said, If it was your story you would have written it.

Oh—it's as simple as that?

Yeah. As simple as that.

By the time I got back to the room after dinner I'd cooled off and was ready to tell Bill my side of things. It wouldn't make us friends, but it might make him understand how the story was really my own. I waited for an hour or so and when he still didn't show up I figured I'd find him in the library.

The scholars' studies were in the basement, five of them awarded to the highest-ranking sixth formers at the start of each year. The basement had its own entrance so they could come and go even when the rest of the library was closed. I didn't like it down there; the air was dead, the long shelves of periodicals depressing in the sheer dusty mass of their obsolescence. The place appeared to be empty that warm May night, no sound at all, no lights showing under the doors. I knocked on Bill's anyway, then tried the handle.

I shouldn't have. I had no business doing that, and no business reading the notebook on his desk. But I took it out of the study and slumped down at the far end of a row of shelves and began to leaf through it under the dim yellow light—over a hundred handwritten pages without a title, without chapters, without any discernible form. I didn't read every word but I read most of it, enough to be overcome by its nakedness and misery and to understand why he could never have shown a page of it to anyone.

After classes that Friday afternoon a boy came to my room and said I should go to the dean's office. I didn't think anything of it. Hemingway would be here the following week, and I assumed Dean Makepeace wanted to give me some tips on how to handle myself with his old friend.

It was hot and steamy. We sixth formers had the privilege of sunbathing on the quad, and at this hour the grass was crowded with pale hairy boys basting themselves with oil as they yelled back and forth over their transistor radios, all tuned to the same station, the same song. I stopped to shoot the breeze with a couple of classmates, then ambled on.

Mrs. Busk, the dean's secretary, was a short woman with a jutting bosom and a scattering of moles across her face. She was leaning out of her office when I arrived, peering down the hallway. Where have you been? she said. They're all waiting.

They?

She went to Dean Makepeace's door and knocked. He's here, she said, then stepped back. Go in.

The headmaster was standing in front of Dean Makepeace's desk. He motioned me to a chair on his left. In the three chairs lined up across from mine sat Mr. Ramsey, Mr. Lambert, and a boy named Goss, president of the Student Honor Council. Mr. Lambert was my French master, a dapper, pipe-smoking Parisian whose collars always looked too tight. Dean Makepeace wasn't there. Despite the air conditioner rattling in one of the windows, the room was hot and Mr. Ramsey's round, ruddy face glistened like a ham.

I didn't know what this was about, but there'd been rumors of cheating on a French final earlier that week. I was clean, and hadn't seen anything that I should have reported.

The headmaster leaned back against the desk and stared at the floor between my feet. He had not looked directly at me since I came in. All right, he said, let's hear it.

Sir?

I'm sure you have a story for us. We're ready to hear it.

It's verr sample, Mr. Lambert said. Tell the truth.

I'm sorry, I said. I don't understand.

You're only making it worse, Goss said. He was a skinny high-voiced boy with one leg in a brace from polio. I'd voted for him, but I didn't like him.

So, the headmaster said. You can think of no reason for our being here today. He kept his eyes on the floor as he spoke. I had the feeling he was deliberately denying me recognition. Usually his brilliant gaze held mine, but in its absence I found myself staring at the wen on his forehead.

Honestly, sir, I'm at a loss.

Hah! Goss said.

Please, Mr. Lambert said to him. *On se calme.*

The headmaster reached across his desk and picked up a piece of paper and handed it to me. It was a photocopy of the first page of "Summer Dance" as it had appeared in *Cantiamo*. The line below the title said *by Susan Friedman*. The name threw me. I'd completely forgotten it. It had flown my mind as soon as I'd begun reading the story that night in the *Troubadour* office and seen my own life laid bare on the page, and in all the time since then I'd never thought of "Summer Dance" as anyone's story but mine.

And I still didn't; not really. Even with the proof in hand, even knowing that someone named Susan Friedman had written the story, I still thought of it as mine. I couldn't reconcile what I knew to be true with what I felt to be true. In fact I couldn't think at all. My eyes moved back and forth between *I hope nobody saw me pick up the cigarette butt*—that sentence that had been so hard to write—and the name above it: Susan Friedman.

Now do you understand why you're here? the headmaster said.

I nodded.

How did this happen? Mr. Ramsey asked. There was no reproach in his tone, only the question itself, and I turned to him with gratitude and the will to give an answer, but none came. I looked at him, then down at the sheet of paper in my hand, my eyes drawn again to that name as if it might yet change back into mine.

Nothing to say? Mr. Lambert said. When I didn't answer, he shrugged and shook his head.

You've dishonored our class, Goss said.

You should know how this came to our attention, the headmaster said. Still looking at the carpet, he explained how the faculty adviser to Miss Cobb's student newspaper came upon "Summer Dance" in her exchange copy of our *News* and immediately recognized it as the story that had caused such a stir at Miss Cobb's some years ago—a dramatic rift between two girls, others taking sides, a great deal of unpleasantness all around.

I tell you this so that you will have at least some inkling of the harm you have caused our school, the headmaster said. This is not a local matter. You have exposed us to contempt and ridicule at least at Miss Cobb's, and far beyond if the story gets out, as it almost certainly will. The newspapers had a carnival last year over the Biltmore incident, and that was nothing compared to this. Mere drunkenness. But this—just watch them. *Ernest Hemingway!* The name is catnip to those people.

He stopped and closed his eyes and pinched the bridge of his nose.

Plagiarism's bad enough, Goss said. But from a girl? I can't believe you'd plagiarize from a girl.

It's a damned good story, Mr. Ramsey said. Whoever wrote it.

Schools like ours are vulnerable to criticism, the headmaster said softly, as if to himself. There is some truth in these criticisms. Too much truth. But we are trying to do something here. We are trying to become something different and even admirable, and for this effort we need all the loyalty we can draw on. More than loyalty. *Love.* It is the love of the old boy for this school that makes everything possible. And how do you think the old boy will feel when he picks up his *Times* or his *Globe* and sees our name associated with a low, shameless, asinine hoax like this? Ernest Hemingway gulled and embarrassed by one of our own!

I'm sorry, I said.

You have no idea of the damage you have done. No idea. Here, already—today. And later to boys such as yourself, and such as I was, boys whose bills are paid by others.

And did we treat you so badly, Mr. Lambert said, that you should think so little of us?

No, sir. Never. I love this school too.

Then I pity your wife and kids, Goss said. If you ever have any.

Enough of that, Mr. Ramsey said.

And what am I to tell Ernest Hemingway, the headmaster said. Good God! He looked at me for the first time. He studied me, up and down. Do you really have nothing to say?

No, sir. Only that I'm sorry.

That may be a good thing for you. It's no use to us. So. Here we are. Mr. Lambert and Mr. Ramsey will collect what you need for the trip home. We'll send the rest on. The train leaves at five. Your father has already been notified.

The class of 1961 is the best class this school ever had, Goss said, and now you've blackened its name.

Oh, please! Mr. Ramsey said.

Goss slouched in his chair.

You understand, the headmaster said, that I will have to advise Columbia that you failed to complete your studies here, and that I cannot vouch for your character. They will withdraw their offer.

Oh.

You do understand? There's to be no confusion about this.

Yes. I understand.

Foolish boy, Mr. Lambert said. I looked at him and saw tears in his eyes.

If after four years with us you could do this, the headmaster said, then you have understood nothing of what we are. You have never really entered the school. So be it. As far as this school is concerned, you were never here.

That is very hard, sir, Mr. Ramsey said.

Do you think so, Mr. Ramsey?

I do.

Maybe you're right. You must do better, he said to me, and walked across the room and out the door.

You're excused—*now*, Mr. Ramsey said to Goss, who'd pushed himself up and turned toward me.

I just wanted to wish him luck. Goss offered me his hand and I disgusted myself by taking it. Well, he said, good luck.

Mr. Lambert followed him to the door and then closed it again.

We'll fill one suitcase and send the rest on, Mr. Ramsey said. Is there anything in particular you need for the trip?

No sir.

Nothing? Mr. Lambert said.

I wanted to ask them to pack my first edition of *In Our Time*, but bringing up Hemingway at just this moment felt like a bad idea. I can't think of anything, I said.

Give Mrs. Busk the combination of your gymnasium locker. We'll clean it out later. Did you have a study?

No.

Please wait here, Mr. Ramsey said.

I sat where they left me. The window was closed but I could still hear shouts and laughter and faint music from the quad. I'd been noticing those sounds from the moment I entered the office, and how they went on no matter what was being said and done in here. They were the sounds I lived with day after day, ordinary and subliminal as my own pulse, yet throughout this meeting I was sharply aware of them, and they distracted me from the actuality of what was happening. During our worst dreams we are assured by a dog barking somewhere, a refrigerator motor kicking on, that we will soon wake to true life. I had somehow—without knowing it—managed to hear such a promise in the hoots and bellows of the boys outside.

Now they sounded different to me. The very heedlessness of their voices defined the distance that had opened up between us. That easy brimming gaiety already seemed impossibly remote, no longer the true life I would wake to each morning, but a paling dream.

My shirt was soaked through. I could smell myself. I got up and prowled the room, looked blindly at the titles of the books on the shelves, then saw two copies of the school paper on the desk. I started reading "Summer Dance," and when the door opened I whipped around like a thief. Mrs. Busk stood in the doorway. Are you all right, dear?

I wasn't sure what she meant. I nodded.

Would you like a glass of apple juice? It's nice and cold.

No, thank you.

They should be back soon.

Yes, ma'am.

All right. Let me know if you want a glass of juice.

When she closed the door again I folded up the paper and put it in my jacket pocket, then sat down to wait.

Mr. Ramsey came back alone. He had my largest suitcase and my overnighter. Mrs. Busk asked me to sign a form of some kind—I didn't read it—and then she followed us to the door of her office. She was actually wringing her hands.

Mr. Ramsey stopped in the hallway. Did you give Mrs. Busk your locker combination, then?

No, not yet.

Well? Mr. Ramsey said.

I'm thinking, I said, but I wasn't thinking; could only look like I was thinking.

That's fine, Mrs. Busk said. Really, dear. It doesn't matter. You can send it along later.

Right, Mr. Ramsey said. Send it later.

His car was parked behind the building. Two younger boys with tennis rackets saw us come out and quickly looked away. The bags, of course. And Mr. Ramsey's spiritless face, if not my own.

We're going to be rather *in anticipo*, Mr. Ramsey said. I thought you'd prefer to spend the extra time at the station. You know, rather than hanging about here.

He drove out on the service road, then took a side street through the village. No other boys saw me leave.

The air was a glaring white haze above the fields. Mr. Ramsey drove as if into a blizzard, slowly, with both hands, peering tensely over the steering wheel. The windows were open and some newspapers on the backseat riffled in the breeze. A pickup truck came up close behind us, dogged us through a series of curves, then made a chancy pass on a short straightaway and barely avoided an oncoming car.

Tell me, Mr. Ramsey said, is that a genuine first edition of *In Our Time?*

I told him it was, and then, unable to stop myself, asked if he'd packed it.

It's in your gladstone. Quite a treasure, that—how'd you come by it?

Gift.

Yes? Well, defend it with your life. It'll make your children rich. *If you have any.* So. You're dead keen on the old bull, aren't you?

He's a great writer.

There are others.

In this century? He's the greatest. Can I ask you a question?

You may.

Why did you censor what he said to you? That wasn't right. You don't censor Ernest Hemingway.

Oh—the blanks. Alumni office. They get the final edit of everything that leaves this school. Didn't know that, did you? The *News* has a big subscriber list. Can't afford to have some captain of industry choke on his biscuit, can we? But I'll admit to some censoring of my own.

A car shot past, horn blaring. Mr. Ramsey honked back, as if to return a greeting.

Mind you, he said, the stuff I left out wouldn't have made it past the vigilance committee, but that's not why I left it out. Let me say that I do not consider Hemingway the greatest writer of this century, but he is a very great writer indeed, and some of what he said to me was unworthy. At his best, he would never have said it—I'm sure of that. It seemed unfair, even mean-spirited, to make such remarks public. In fact we probably shouldn't have run the interview at all.

You had no right to touch a word of his. It was wrong.

What I cut would've been cut anyway. But I certainly take your point.

Was it about my story?

Susan Friedman's story, I believe you mean. No. My God, no. Everything but. I'm not sure *what* it was about, except his own unhappiness. He is not a happy man. He is like the wounded lion in "Macomber," flexing his claws, looking to take some heads off.

It was still wrong, I said.

This is hardly the time for you to instruct me on a point of honor. Let it go, for Christ's sake!

Yes, *sir*, I said, and turned toward the fields.

Sorry, he said. He drove in silence a while, then said, Strange word, honor—can't be spoken aloud, turns immediately to bilge. Hemingway had that right.

You don't believe in the Honor Code?

That's not what I said. But no, certainly not. Send a boy packing if he breaks the rules, by all means. Plant a boot on his backside, but do please leave the word *honor* out of it. It's disgusting, how we forever throw it about.

I was shocked. I didn't see how the school could work without the Honor Code, and I said so.

Make good rules and hold the boys to them. No need to be pawing at their souls. Honor Code? Pretentious nonsense.

We were in town now. This gave Mr. Ramsey occasion to go even slower. I watched myself in the storefront windows as we crept along, appearing and vanishing and appearing again. The few people on the street had a squinty, peevish look, but their ignorance of my situation made me feel thankful to them. For once I was glad for how big the world was. And this somehow gave me heart to ask the question I'd been circling ever since we left the school.

What did my father say?

Pardon?

What did my father say when he heard . . . you know.

Ah. He didn't believe it. Told the headmaster we didn't know a thing about you if we thought you'd do anything on the cheat, that you were the most honest person he knew.

He said that?

So I understand. Gave the headmaster an earful. All but called him a liar.

We got to the station well before my train. Mr. Ramsey went to the ticket counter while I waited on the platform with my bags. An old woman in a black dress and white bonnet kept inching up to the edge to peer down the track. Two redcaps stood by their carts in the shade behind my bench, talking in low voices, as if in deference to the heat. Otherwise I was alone on the platform, until Mr. Ramsey came out of the waiting room with my ticket.

He waved off my thanks. Your father will get the bill soon enough. I'll wait with you, if you don't mind.

You don't have to.

He lowered himself to the bench and closed his eyes and leaned back so the sun fell full on his face. Without opening his eyes he fumbled in the pockets of his wrinkled linen jacket, produced a pack of Gitanes, shook out a cigarette, then tipped the pack toward me as if I were not a boy of the school. I couldn't bring myself to take one.

How come Dean Makepeace wasn't there? I said.

Mr. Ramsey put the cigarettes back in his pocket. He didn't answer.

He's the dean. Why didn't he throw me out?

Dean Makepeace left school this morning. Mr. Lambert has stepped in as dean pro tem.

What, he just left?

He had some personal matters to attend to, I believe.

So he'll miss seeing Hemingway.

Yes, I suppose he will.

We fell into a long silence then. I didn't mind not talking. I was at ease with Mr. Ramsey because he hadn't crowed or condescended, and also because I knew Mrs. Ramsey had carried on a flirtation with Bill White that year. I knew this from reading Bill's notebook, a wail of longing so raw that he hadn't bothered to change or disguise her name. He addressed her directly, as we argue and plead and rebuke while pacing a room alone. By turns cold, gushy, furious, pained, and punishingly repetitive, these pages had not been written to be read. Bill would never let himself be seen like this.

He referred to her kisses and described them in lingering detail, but nothing more, and I figured there was nothing more to describe or he would have done it in these unguarded pages. I couldn't make out exactly what had happened, though I could guess how it started—the two of them talking, kidding around when Mrs. Ramsey came down to the library basement to file some periodicals, an impulsive kiss in the stacks, then other kisses, maybe even in Bill's study. It was a schoolboy fantasy—one of my own, in fact—come true. Until Mrs. Ramsey woke up and ended it.

I suspected that Mr. Ramsey knew. It was just a feeling I had. But whether he knew or not, I did; and this somehow allowed me to be easy in his presence.

The platform began to fill. The old woman in the white bonnet came over to show us her ticket and ask if her train had already come and gone without her. I told her it was my train too, and that it hadn't yet arrived. A little while later I saw her showing her ticket to another man.

Mr. Ramsey bent forward and rubbed his eyes. What will you do? he said.

I don't know.

Of course. Quite right, too. But you might . . . Then he stopped and never finished the thought.

When the train came he lugged my suitcase on board and put it in the luggage rack at the end of the car. I followed him out to the vestibule and we shook hands.

Here one says something, he said. It's not the end of the world, be game, you'll work things out . . . But for all I know you won't work things out. How should I know? He patted his pockets for the Gitanes, put one in his mouth, and offered another to me. When I hesitated he stuck the pack in my shirt pocket and stepped down onto the platform and walked away, two long sweat stains darkening the back of his jacket. I was glad to see him go; several minutes still remained before departure time and I'd worried he might stand vigil outside, watching me through the window and giving sad little nods whenever our eyes met.

A steady line of wilted-looking passengers jostled past me into the carriage. Time to make a move. I pushed through to a forward-facing window seat, claimed it with my overnighter—my gladstone—took out In Our Time, and made my way to the smoking car.

ONE FOR
THE BOOKS

I didn't go home. Instead I got off the train in New York and cashed in the rest of my ticket and took a room at the Y. The *Times* wasn't hiring reporters with my qualifications, nor were any of the other papers. They wouldn't even take me on as a copyboy. I finally landed a job busing tables at a cheap tourist restaurant near Times Square, along with half a bedroom in the headwaiter's nearby apartment, where two other waiters bunked in the living room. All three came from Ecuador. Since they didn't speak much English and I spoke no Spanish, they mostly behaved as if I wasn't there. So did I.

This is the job I had when Ernest Hemingway killed himself. He never did visit my school; too sick to travel. Afterward I worked as a room service waiter at the Pierre, as a restaurant waiter, a picture framer, and, for a short time, a Brinks guard; then, for an even shorter time, as a plumber's assistant, and again as a waiter. I wrote some wiseguy features for an allegedly hip tourist mag that quickly folded, moved five or six times, drank a lot, had a few good friends and one girlfriend as faithless as I tried to be, read many books, signed up for extension courses at the New School and dropped them all. After almost three years of this I enlisted in the army and ended up in Vietnam.

If this looks like a certain kind of author's bio, that's no accident. Even as I lived my life I was seeing it on the back of a book. And yet in all those years I actually wrote very little, maybe because I was afraid of not being good enough to justify this improvised existence, and because the improvising became an end in itself and left scant room for disciplined invention.

A more truthful dust-jacket sketch would say that the author, after much floundering, went to college and worked like the drones he'd once despised, kept reasonable hours, learned to be alone in a room, learned to throw stuff out, learned to keep gnawing the same bone until it cracked. It would say that the author lived more like a banker than an outlaw and that his deepest pleasures were familial—hearing his wife sing as she worked in the garden, unzipping her dress after a party; seeing his most solemn child laugh at something he said. The brief years of friendship with his father before he died, never once allowing that his son had anything to be pardoned for.

It would be very boring. It would also be pointless, merely incidental rather than exemplary. For a writer there is no such thing as an exemplary life. It's a fact that certain writers do good work at the bottom of a bottle. The outlaws generally write as well as the bankers, though more briefly. Some writers flourish like opportunistic weeds by hiding among the citizens, others by toughing it out in one sort of desert or another.

The life that produces writing can't be written about. It is a life carried on without the knowledge even of the writer, below the mind's business and noise, in deep unlit shafts where phantom messengers struggle toward us, killing one another along the way; and when a few survivors break through to our attention they are received as blandly as waiters bringing more coffee.

No true account can be given of how or why you became a

writer, nor is there any moment of which you can say: This is when I became a writer. It all gets cobbled together later, more or less sincerely, and after the stories have been repeated they put on the badge of memory and block all other routes of exploration. There's something to be said for this. It's efficient, and may even provide a homeopathic tincture of the truth.

Here is one such story of my own.

In the fall of 1965 I got orders for a training course at Fort Holabird, Maryland. As I cleaned out my billet before leaving Fort Bragg I came across the copy of the *News* I'd taken from the dean's office the day of my expulsion. I lay back on my bunk and read the story through for the first time in years. It held up well, I thought, but I was no longer in any confusion as to whose story it was, or whose talent Hemingway had blessed. I assumed that Susan Friedman had been told what I'd done. To square things a little, at least with myself, I wrote a brief note of apology and mailed it to her, along with the *News*, in care of Miss Cobb's alumnae office.

Damn if she didn't write back. *Plagiarism, not imitation, is the sincerest form of flattery*, she wrote, and thanked me for the further compliment of showing her work to Ernest Hemingway. *So old Hairy Chest liked it!* No one at Miss Cobb's had given her any hint of this distinction; not, she added cryptically, that *this* came as any surprise. She found the whole thing a fantastic lark, and thanked me again for letting her in on it.

Then, in a postscript: *I see you used your own first name in the story, but kept Levine. Interesting touch.*

That seemed to invite a response. Her return address was in Washington, D.C., less than an hour away, so why not answer her in person? For days I fretted over my next letter, trying to find the exact tone, witty but not frivolous, that would make Susan Friedman accept my invitation to dinner—*in partial payment*, as I expressed it, *of my debt*. Within an hour of posting the letter I was writhing at its juvenility. She wouldn't even answer. But she did, and said that while nights were difficult she might manage lunch sometime. This sounded like a brush-off, except that she included her telephone number.

We agreed to meet at an Italian restaurant on Wisconsin Avenue. I got there early and Susan was late, so I had plenty of time to pass from elation to despair, as I'd been doing all week. What did I hope for, to be in such a state? I pretended to hope for nothing, just a good meal and some interesting talk, but I couldn't fool myself. This meeting felt momentous to me, it had the potential of making sense of the maze I'd wandered into when I chanced upon her story. Suppose—a ridiculous supposition, I knew, but just suppose—we fell in love and ended up together. Then it would turn out to have been something more than bad luck that led me to "Summer Dance," and all the confusions since would be revealed as cunning arabesques in a most intricate, beautifully formed story.

I knew I should keep my feet on the ground, knew that my enforced isolation from women had made me vulnerable to runaway dreams. But we already had so much in common—the same story, so to speak. I had liked her voice when I called to arrange lunch: cool and low, with an elusive teasing quality. She'd laughed at odd times as we talked, and this flustered me pleasantly, and made me laugh too, as if we both understood something we couldn't say.

She was very late. I nursed a beer and looked over the lunch menu, surprisingly cheap for such a busy, sunny place, with snowy tablecloths and heavy silver and real Italian waiters in black vests. I guessed she'd suggested it to save me money, and for this I was both pleased and suspicious of condescension. Now and then my waiter glanced at me and I smarted under his gaze. He was young and roosterish and I knew what he was thinking—that I'd been stood up and might as well admit it and either order up or scram. But I held out, and then she was coming toward me, pulling off her gloves. She had a slightly cleft chin and straight dark hair cut in an old-fashioned bob and wore the black overcoat and red scarf she said she'd be wearing. Her color was high. She seemed to bring with her some of the crispness of that fine November day. She gave the waiter her coat and scarf and we shook hands and sat down together.

I expected her to make some excuse for being late but instead she reached into her purse and brought out a pack of Luckies. This is one for the books, she said, and laughed. Having lunch with my own personal plagiarist.

I lit her cigarette. She stopped my wrist with her hand and my breath caught, but she just wanted to see the lighter. She turned it over, squinted at the unit insignia on its side, then fished a pair of glasses from her purse and studied it again. She had a soft fleshy prettiness like girls in silent films, and the clunky black frames of her glasses did not make her any less pretty, only more vivid, as she certainly knew. Hmm, she said, and handed the lighter back and turned that studying gaze on me. I saw that she had a lazy eye.

You don't look anything like I thought you would, she said.

Neither do you, I said, in revenge, but it was true. I had thought of her as leaner, sharper, a little wolfish.

I won't ask what you were expecting, she said.

Then I won't either.

Do they make you cut your hair like that?

Yes, but it isn't much different from the way I used to wear it.

That's okay, she said. I don't like long hair on men.

She asked me about the unit I served with and why I'd joined

the army. I picked my way through the answer, afraid of striking a false note. My carefulness bored her. She glanced over the
menu while I trailed off.

Then I said, it's something I thought I should do.

For God and country, she said, eyes still on the menu.

No. It was an expectation I had of myself. I would have
always felt like I'd missed a base if I hadn't done it.

I'm going to have the tuna salad. She put the menu down and
looked at me. Why do you think you had that expectation?

When I told her I didn't exactly know she laughed and said,
You don't exactly know. Well, I do.

But when I asked her what she knew she smiled like a big sister holding something over her little brother's head, just out of
reach, and would not tell me.

And that was how it went from there. My case was hopeless.
Susan had five years on me, which didn't have to mean anything
in itself, but did mean something because of what she'd done
with that time. From Miss Cobb's she got a free ride to Wellesley
but dropped out after a semester when her mother was diagnosed
with cancer. Susan looked after her sister and their mother until
she died two years later, then worked at different jobs while fin-
ishing her degree. She didn't return to Wellesley; she went to
Ohio State to stay closer to her sister, and was now in her second year at Georgetown Medical School. I saw that she was an
extraordinary person, and that I had nothing to offer her but an
hour or so of good company, which proved easier once I no longer
felt the tension of hope.

As we ate lunch we talked about our schooldays. Susan took
a hard view of Miss Cobb's and also of my own school, which she
remembered well from joint concerts and dances: boys dropping
hints of their importance within moments of meeting her, then
triangulating her own position from an unvarying progress of

questions about friends, parties, and vacations; boys forcing themselves on her as if she had no choice in the matter and then, if she held them off, exchanging signs with other boys to be relieved of her, even on occasion abandoning her on the dance floor; their refusal to discover whether she could think or even talk; their transparent designs and appalling confidence.

Susan considered my caper with her story a fine joke on this ivy-covered stud farm, and on Papa, as she acidly called him, and on the idea of literature as some kind of great phallic enterprise like bullfighting or boxing. Change a few names and pronouns and Papa himself, the peerless measurer of penises—why the funny face? Hadn't I read *A Moveable Feast?*—Papa himself couldn't tell if he was reading the story of a boy or a girl. So much for the supreme arbiter of manhood, not to mention his built-in shit detector! And so much for the supposedly basic differences between the sexes by which our schools justified their absurd existences.

It was a *terrific* prank, she said. But what in the world made you think of it?

This put me in a corner. I understood that whatever curiosity had drawn her to this lunch hinged on her belief that all these subversions were deliberate. What would she think if I told her I'd loved both Hemingway and my school, and that playing them for fools had never crossed my mind? How could I explain that it hadn't been just Ernest Hemingway but I myself who couldn't tell us apart?

It was all too complicated, and hardly plausible—less so than Susan's version, to which, I sensed, she was attached with a ferocity I shouldn't provoke. With a modest shrug, I let things stand.

You used your own name, she said. That's smart, that always gets them eating out of your hand. You kept Levine, though. I guess you needed a Jewish name for the story to work, but still. You're not Jewish, are you?

Good question, I said. It depends on what you mean by Jewish. Here at last I gathered myself to do some truth-telling, but Susan cut me off with a laugh.

Son, if it depends on what I mean by Jewish, then you're not Jewish. She turned and signaled the waiter. Sorry, she said, I've got a heavy date with Agnes. She laughed again when she saw my face. My cadaver.

Oh.

Anyway, I'm flattered that you put my poor effort to such good use.

It isn't a poor effort. It's a fine story.

Nah. It's a well-written little exercise in unhappiness and spite, that's all.

It's not just well written. It's brave and honest.

How do you know it's honest?

I looked at her.

How do you know it isn't a sham from start to finish?

I guess I don't.

The waiter came with the bill and gave it to Susan. He didn't even glance in my direction. Please, I said, this is on me.

She counted some bills onto the table. Gotta support the troops. She must have sensed my humiliation, because she reached over and gave my hand a squeeze. You get the next one, she said, though I knew there wouldn't be a next one. Tell me, you really did like that story?

It's terrific. I'd read anything by you.

There's nothing to read.

You don't write?

Not for years.

That's sad.

Not at all.

Well, it makes me sad.

You'll pull through. She stood up, and I stood with her. The waiter helped her on with her coat and when she said *mille grazie* he all but purred. We walked outside and stopped in front of the restaurant. Susan gave me a hug. You be careful, she said.

Is it a sham?

Must dash, she said.

You should keep writing.

Mmm, don't think so. Too frivolous. Know what I mean? It just cuts you off and makes you selfish and doesn't really do any good.

This actually shocked me. We know what is sacred to us when we recoil from impiety, and Susan's casual desertion of her gift had exactly that force. She saw I was about to say something. Just one gal's opinion, she said, and waggled her fingers and headed up the street.

I visited a couple of bars on M Street and worked up my answer to Susan. By the time I got back to the barracks that night I had it cold: Her problem was not with writing but with men. Her patricidal tone when she said *Papa*—some interesting bitterness there. And though she ridiculed the notion of literature as a phallic enterprise, she obviously suffered from that confusion herself. The problem was how she looked at things. The fact that a writer needed solitude didn't mean he was cut off or selfish. A writer was like a monk in his cell praying for the world—something he performed alone, but for other people.

Then to say it did no good! How could she say that? Of course it did good. And I stood there half-drunk and adrift in this bay of snoring men, and gave thanks for all the good it had done me.

BULLETIN

I figured the school had washed its hands of me, spat me out for good, but eventually the Old Boys' office got my range and started pumping out the alumni bulletins. Over the years they invited me to reunions and glee-club concerts and championship hockey games and archaeological cruises in the Aegean; asked me to send in poignant memories of a retiring master, news of recent successes for the class notes.

I never made it to these musters of the corps, nor advertised my progress, but I read every bulletin from cover to cover. Thus I learned of Jack Broome's death while landing his A6 on an aircraft carrier, and of George Kellogg's Rhodes Scholarship and his march through the philosophy departments of Penn and Yale and Stanford. Purcell sent nothing in, but Big Jeff did, regularly. He'd gone into computers early on and now had his own famous company. In one of his postings he included a picture of two men standing before a background of distant mountains. The caption read: *Cousin Roundup! Big Boots and Little Boots Purcell, '61, on Little Boots's ranch in Idaho. Ride them dogies!* Big Jeff had his arm around Purcell's shoulder and was smiling with undisguised love. Purcell looked stoical. He was whip-thin and his face had gotten long and bony. An interesting face. I considered getting in touch by sending him the *In Our Time* he'd given me, but didn't. I never saw a word about Bill White.

Dean Makepeace died of a heart attack in 1967 while walking to class. He was sixty-nine. It surprised me to read in the memorial issue that he had recently married one of the school secretaries. I didn't recognize her in the cover photograph, a plump woman with big round glasses sitting beside him in the football stadium, a single plaid blanket on their knees, both of them yelling and waving pennants. I spent long minutes over that picture—Dean Makepeace carried away by a woman and a game! The article mentioned his service in Italy during World War I, and ran a sepia picture of a lean, unsmiling young soldier in puttees standing beside an ambulance. He had come to the school in 1930 and taught there ever since, except for a leave of absence in '61–'62, the year after my expulsion. *Generations of boys,* the piece concluded, *will never forget his kindness in times of need, even as they quake to recall the famous Blue Gaze falling on them in class, and the inevitable question: And you—what do you think?*

The headmaster retired in 1968, was replaced by a man from Exeter who left after just two years, and then Mr. Ramsey became headmaster. It was he who arranged the so-called partnership with the failing Miss Cobb's Academy, which for all practical purposes ceased to exist. Now our mud-caked quarterbacks shared the bulletin's photo spread with girls sliding into home, lunging for the heart with fencing foils, and crossing the stage on graduation day to rake in the prizes. It was Mr. Ramsey who started the exchange programs with schools in St. Petersburg and Tokyo. And who, not long ago, invited me back as a visiting writer.

When the invitation came I felt an almost embarrassing sense of relief. I didn't know I was waiting for it, though I must have been. But then I had second thoughts; I couldn't make up my mind to accept. My family urged me on. Of course I should go! How could I pass up the chance to return in honor to a place I'd left in disgrace? As a writer, how could I refuse to bring the story to so satisfying and shapely a close?

Maybe that shapely close was part of what held me back. The appetite for decisive endings, even the belief that they're possible, makes me uneasy in life as in writing, and may have accounted for some of the dread I felt at the thought of going back.

That fine *pensée* arrived after the fact. The excuse I gave myself at the time was that someday I'd write something about my days at the school, and needed to guard my fragile vision of the place. Memory is a dream to begin with, and what I had was a dream of memory, not to be put to the test.

All of which made a perverse kind of sense and helped distract me from a deeper unease, humiliating to consider: Would I have been invited at all if I were not one of the school's own? When I thought of the writers I'd seen there as a boy I felt chastened and shy. Did I really own a place among them? If we were all assembled for some great feast, would I be taken for a waiter?

Too much room for doubt. Suspicion of bias—unwitting, patriotic bias—would shadow every moment of my visit. There'd be a stir when I appeared in the dining hall, quite possibly an ovation. Mr. Ramsey would offer celebratory remarks before my talk and faculty members would make haste to welcome the prodigal home; and under it all would run a spirit of amazed, hilarious congratulation that would give me no end of pleasure if only I could believe I'd earned it. Otherwise I'd feel an imposter. Feel only my deficits, and my distance from those I admired.

All vanity, of course. I knew it was vain, even yellow, to decline; but I declined, pleading a full calendar. My family was disgusted.

The following spring I met Mr. Ramsey by chance in the lobby of the Alexis in Seattle. I had arrived that morning for a friend's funeral and was coming in from a late dinner when I saw him talking to the night clerk and, despite his white hair, recognized him instantly. For a moment I considered going on to the elevator, but there are limits to anyone's cowardice and instead I waited until he finished his business at the desk. As he turned away I said, Hello, Mr. Ramsey.

He stopped and lowered his head, peering at me over the top of his glasses. You! he said.

We went into the little bar off the lobby and took the table in back. Mr. Ramsey had just hosted a fund-raising dinner for local alums, the last of a long string of them on the West Coast, and was clearly giddy with exhaustion and relief. He wore a white dinner jacket as shapeless and woebegone as the linen jacket I'd last seen him in. The boyish flush in his cheeks had overspread his entire face and crimsoned his snub, puggish nose. As we drank and talked he continued to study me over his glasses, so smudged they barely reflected the light.

Mr. Ramsey didn't mention my declining to visit the school, but every other subject felt like a dodge. Finally I broke off and said, Look, I'm sorry I let you down.

He finished his scotch and savored it a moment. Did you let me down?

I should've accepted your invitation.

Ah. Well, of course we all wish you had. A busy time for you. Can't be helped.

Still, I should have come.

He said nothing.

You may not remember, I said, but when you took me to the station you gave me a pack of Gitanes.

Gitanes! What wouldn't I do for one now, eh? Wife made me quit—bad role-modeling. Nation of scolds. But yes, I remember every godawful moment of that day. You don't know the half of it.

Oh?

Hell of a story, actually.

The ability to order another round without anyone but the waitress noticing is, if not a danger sign, a handy talent, and Mr. Ramsey had it. But I was disappointed when after the fuss of taking delivery he didn't pick up where he left off. Instead he asked about my twin daughters and my son. When he heard they were all in college he wanted to know why I'd never sent them to him.

I could've used the girls, he said.

It never crossed our minds.

I do hope it wasn't money. I have oodles of money and can give it to anyone I like.

Well, it would've been a consideration if we'd thought about boarding school. But we liked having them around.

Really. Most laudable, I'm sure. No hard feelings, then?

What—toward the school?

You did get the bum's rush. Cursed to the tenth generation. We do things differently now.

No hard feelings. On the contrary.

Good! Then why didn't you come back?

I sensed that Mr. Ramsey would not find thin-sliced arguments about the delicacy of memory very satisfying. So I took my heart in my hands and described the recurrent vision of being called to a feast with all these writers, and then discovering after so many years of work—work which had indeed cut me off, and given pain to others—that I had no place at the table.

You underestimate us, Mr. Ramsey said. I have the seating

chart well in hand. We will put you between Ayn Rand and Ernest Hemingway's empty chair.

Was this a joke or some complicated critique? I felt my brow knot up.

So you will come?

Yes, I said, I'm almost sure I can come. I let a moment pass, then said: You mentioned a story.

He allowed me a fleeting smile. There is a problem of confidentiality. I can rely on your discretion?

No.

Mr. Ramsey appeared to mull this over, but I knew he would tell me, just as I knew he would first justify telling me, and so he did. The person in question, he said, never desired this secrecy; it was enjoined upon him. He would have wanted the truth to be known. Finally, one does want to be known.

The story concerned Dean Makepeace. Arch, as Mr. Ramsey called him, had befriended him and the first Mrs. Ramsey early on, when most other masters and their wives held back. In those days the school did not open its arms to newcomers. And it could be especially cold to a young master who didn't hide his somewhat garish light under a bushel. But Arch liked talking about books and ideas, and could still give up old ground for new, whereas his fellow masters had generally made up their minds about things. He forgave Mr. Ramsey his impudence because Mr. Ramsey did not bore him.

They became friends—the unhappy young couple and Arch Makepeace, who, when he joined them for drinks or Sunday dinner, somehow filled the distance between them, as Mr. Ramsey supposed a child might have done. Arch *was* something of a child, and Roberta treated him like one, fussing over him, chiding him tenderly, cooking his favorite dishes and watching his face for the least sign of pleasure. Their marriage would not have lasted as long as it did without him. And when it did end, when Roberta left, it was Arch Makepeace who held Mr. Ramsey together, changing overnight from child to father.

For two months he walked Mr. Ramsey through his life. He stopped by on his way to breakfast to get him out of bed and see that he made himself presentable, and more often than not helped him back into bed at night after listening to hours of accusation and complaint. When Mr. Ramsey had a pugilistic adventure with a Brit-baiting Irishman in Boston, Arch bailed him out and put his friendship with the headmaster at risk by concealing the incident. He listened, and listened, and listened, and never once reproached Mr. Ramsey with useless truths or tried to cheer him up.

So I could probably imagine how Mr. Ramsey received the news that Arch Makepeace, after thirty years at the school, had in the span of a single morning decided to leave. And not an hour later Mr. Ramsey was summoned to review the evidence against me and to participate in my expulsion. Oh, how he hated these Danny Deever events—*nine 'undred of 'is county an' the regiment's disgrace*, et cetera.

In fact he already knew I would be expelled, because Arch had told him as much when he said his good-bye. I should not flatter myself that Dean Makepeace had given up his work and home in protest at my well-earned dismissal, but the two things were connected in a very curious way. Which brought us to his story.

Mr. Ramsey had been leaning forward as he talked. Now he stopped as if to consider the ground ahead. He settled back and allowed me to see that he was not a young man, and that he was very tired, and that going on would be an effort.

Then he went on, holding still in his chair and telling the story from that distance. Everything Mr. Ramsey said interested me, and much of it surprised me, including my own obliviously decisive role in this drama. He kept it short, but in the submerged-iceberg manner he used to mock, so that I was somehow given to know more than was actually said. The spaces he left empty began filling up even as he spoke.

He didn't quite finish. While describing Dean Makepeace's wedding he broke off and pushed himself forward and called *Price! Price!* to a bald, blackbearded man in a dinner jacket who'd just come into the bar and was scowling around. Mr. Ramsey introduced us and said that Mr. Price, the senior history master, had presented another of his *brilliant* lectures and slideshows at that evening's dinner.

Yeah, yeah, Mr. Price said.

On what subject? I asked.

School history—what else?

Mr. Ramsey declared his great coup in persuading me to come for a visit.

Oh, at last, Mr. Price said. Can't wait. He turned to Mr. Ramsey. How'd we do tonight? Did you manage to collar that little shit Armentrout?

Of course.

I saw him going all out for the exit, him and that scarlet fright-wig on his arm.

Mrs. Armentrout has been a great support to our Ned.

How much you get out of him?

Forty.

Forty? After the windfall he had? The old man left him everything! Forty? That *dress* of hers cost forty.

With a promise to reconsider if the market improves.

We should've given him the boot that time. You remember—him down on his warty little knees blubbering for a second chance. Tear up the check. Forty is an insult.

I will bear it.

What about Melissa Didget?

On and on they went. I didn't feel slighted by their inattention, not at all. It left me free to contemplate the story I'd just been told; and anyway, I liked listening in, feeling the same illicit pleasure I'd known as a boy when the masters forgot my presence and unsheathed their tongues. It was a kind of music they made, and it carried me back to those Sunday teas in the headmaster's parlor, red leaves or snow or whirling maple seeds falling past the tall windows. The great Persian rug is covered with cookie crumbs. The air smells of the Greek master's cigar. In the far corner someone plays "Beautiful Dreamer" on the tinkly upright, fragments of the melody floating just above our voices. We boys stand in circles and trade witty remarks, all the while straining to catch what the masters are saying that makes them laugh so easily, so unguardedly. The boy closest to them smiles into his punch glass. He can hear them; he has slipped into their camp and can hear the secret music of these sure and finished men, our masters.

MASTER

The problem started at one of the headmaster's teas, when a boy asked Arch if he had known Ernest Hemingway during World War I. The room was crowded and noisy, and Arch distracted, so later he couldn't recall exactly how he'd answered but came to accept that he had not been clear in his denial.

He understood how the question arose. Hemingway had driven an ambulance in Italy, as he had, and both had suffered leg injuries. But they'd never met. Hemingway served with the Red Cross, Arch with the Army Ambulance Service. And they got hurt in very different circumstances—Hemingway while carrying a wounded man under fire, Arch in a stupid accident. The fuel line of his ambulance fed off a gravity tank. The engine tended to stall out on steep grades unless you drove backward uphill, and that's what Arch was doing in late October of 1918, driving backward over a mountain pass near Cima Grappa, when a staff car surprised him in a tight corner and he jerked the wheel too hard and backed right off the road. His partner was thrown out immediately and walked away with a few bruises, but Arch got caught inside and rolled down into the trees like a pea in a can and ended up with a broken arm, a broken collarbone, two broken

179

wrists, a badly sprained neck, and a shattered knee. Those were the serious injuries. The others looked worse, but within a few weeks he could face a mirror without despair. The medicos did a good job on him. Everything healed up except the knee, which never worked right again and gave him more and more trouble as time went on, until he finally gave in and got himself a cane whose evident cheapness inspired the graduating class of 1939 to present him with a fine blackthorn stick, silver-handled.

He knew that his limp interested the boys, but he didn't talk about it because he disliked recalling his panic and incompetence. Arch Makepeace was not a man to tell stories on himself. Though he hadn't intended his silence to mean anything, from his first days at the school people drew certain conclusions from it that gave him an authority he wouldn't otherwise have enjoyed.

It proved useful. Willful boys who would've felt obliged to test another master gave Arch a pass. The masters themselves—none of whom actually made it to Europe during the war, though some had been in uniform—treated him from the beginning with a respect it would have taken anyone else years to squeeze out of them. Arch didn't like to think that this consideration depended on a misunderstanding, but that was no fault of his. He had never lied about his experience. If the speculations of others brought out the best in them, let them speculate.

The business about Hemingway was different. One night a boy at his table asked him if Hemingway had gone over to the Bolshies in Spain. Arch just stared at him, trying to understand the reason for this question. It was 1947. The Spanish civil war had ended eight years ago and since then another world war had been fought. Arch was thinking: Why this question, now? The boy flushed and looked down as if he'd been judged impertinent. Over dinner the awkwardness passed, but Arch found the moment troubling. Why would the boy ask *him* about Ernest Hemingway's beliefs? And why would he then feel, as he so obviously did, that he had presumed on Arch by asking, as though the question were somehow too personal? Then Arch remembered the other boy's question at the headmaster's tea some weeks back and wondered if he had made himself clear, and knew that he had not.

He experienced kindred moments in the following years, though not many and never of a kind that gave him license to say, What the deuce are you talking about? I've never laid eyes on Ernest Hemingway! Word had probably gone out that he could not be approached on the subject of Hemingway the man, though Hemingway the writer had an important place in his honors seminar on contemporary literature. The boys were politic. They had been bred to conceal their interest in famous names, but by an elusive, delicately shaded remark they might still hint at some privileged awareness, and Arch caught enough of these—just a hint here and there, never an opening for decisive refutation—to recognize that the boys believed that he and Hemingway were friends.

Arch had left room for doubt that day at the headmaster's tea, and he knew why, or thought he did: some hidden yearning to be part of the great world. To be important, even by association.

He didn't see this as a lie so much as a kind of dozing off in his attention to the truth. And he was attentive to the truth. The truth wanted to be sought after but it would let itself be seen now and then, and this happened to Arch most often while he was teaching. He'd been a reader since childhood, and the habit had deepened during his years of travel for the Forbes-Farragut shipping line, but until he began teaching he'd rarely had occasion to talk about what he read. He could read a story like "The Minister's Black Veil" and both shrink from and relish the soul-chill it worked on him without having to fix that response in words, or explain how Hawthorne had produced it. Teaching made him accountable for his thoughts, and as he became accountable for them he had more of them, and they became sharper and deeper. It was the nature of literature to behave like the fallen world it contemplated, this dusky ground where subterfuge reigns and certainty is folly, and Arch felt like some master of hounds as he led the boys deep into a story or poem, driving them on with questions, forcing them to test cadence, gesture, and inflection for feint and doubletalk until at last the truth showed its face for an instant before vanishing into some new possibility of meaning. He sometimes arrived at the end of a class dripping with sweat, hardly knowing where he was or how long he'd been there, all his damned dignity gone.

Arch hadn't meant to teach. In fact he used to wonder with a stern kind of pity how his own teachers, especially the ones he looked up to, had allowed themselves to become schoolbound. But just three years after he got married his wife failed to return from a trip to California, and then Forbes-Farragut went under in the general havoc, and he couldn't for the life of him find work until his old roommate from Cornell invited Arch to apply for the job he planned to vacate—teaching America's heirs presumptive what the *tempus fugit* on their grandfather clocks meant. Although Arch had taken his degree in classics he didn't get that job, but just before school started they offered him another, teaching English. He came with the intention of leaving at the end of the year but stayed on for another, and then another. This seemed to happen naturally, without any effort of decision, but of course Arch had his reasons, and he knew that comfort and habit were among them, and probably counted for more than they should. But he also believed that his teaching was good—good for the boys and good for him, making him more alert and self-forgetful and more truthful.

So he hunched up a little when something reminded him of this myth about Makepeace and Hemingway. But it didn't happen very often, and God knows he had other things to think

about. Arch taught a full schedule of classes and because he had
no family at school he volunteered for more than his share of
committee work. His wife, Helen, lived out west, but they had
never divorced and in her many troubles she did not hesitate to
call on him for help. Sometimes it was just his sympathy she
wanted, for bad health or bad luck or mistreatment by one of her
friends, as she called them. She took small loans from Arch and
usually paid them back. Helen wasn't a mean or scheming person
but things tended to get away from her. When the riding stable
she managed in Palm Springs threatened her with charges over a
problem in their accounts, Arch helped defray the shortfall and
obtain mercy from the owner. Later on he performed the same
office with a stable in Tucson. She moved often. He lost track
of her for longer and longer periods, and these silences worried
him more than her recurrent needs and complaints. The beautiful, lippy, headlong Kentucky girl Arch had married became a
woman of no fixed address. She was killed in Phoenix early one
morning in 1953 while walking across an intersection against the
light. Her friend of the moment didn't tell Arch for two months,
and then only because he needed the money he'd spent on her
cremation to pay off a pressing debt. Arch hoped it was a hustle,
but the funeral home confirmed the man's story and sent along a
copy of Helen's death certificate.

That was the same year he became dean. The new headmaster had some changes in mind and relied on Arch, his former
colleague in the English faculty, to back him up in contests with
recalcitrant masters and alumni. Moneychangers called Arch
straight from their tables in the Temple to protest the end of
compulsory religious education. When the headmaster moved
to divert more of the endowment into scholarship funds, two
trustees resigned and sent out a letter arguing that if this sort of
thing kept up, the school they knew and loved—which wasn't,
after all, a *public* school—would be altered beyond recognition.

The headmaster prevailed, but just barely, and Arch knew that his support had made the difference. At crucial moments, strong, difficult men had deferred to him.

And why did he have that power? Being dean cut no ice; deans came and went. Arch considered himself a good teacher, yet so were other masters who wouldn't have carried the day. He suspected that it had something to do with this Hemingway business. The school had its names, to be sure, its giants of commerce, its cabinet officers, ambassadors and generals, even a long-dead president, but none of these names had real magic. Arch sensed that through him the school felt itself connected to a greatness radiant with glamour, as if he were at once their own Archibald Makepeace, master and dean, and also Frederick Henry and Nick Adams and Robert Jordan and Jake Barnes and Ernest Hemingway himself, all mystically present in him and adding their consequence to his. He hoped he had this wrong, but thought he probably had it right.

Arch dropped *A Farewell to Arms* from his honors seminar because he feared that all this wounded-ambulance-driver stuff might encourage the confusion, but he always kept something by Hemingway on his reading list. Though he didn't love Hemingway as he loved Hawthorne and Melville and Edith Wharton and F. Scott Fitzgerald, he admired him and understood how others could love him. Love him as a writer, that is. Arch had lost interest in Hemingway himself long ago, and wished everyone else would lose interest too, as in the normal course of things one would.

This was not to be. Other reputations bloomed and faded, but not this one. Every year it grew brighter, and the man himself more of a figure, and harder to separate from the work. He loomed over it; Arch could almost feel him drawing up into himself the love and honor he demanded for his characters. Who could not think of Hemingway when reading about Colonel Cantwell pissing on the Italian battleground where he'd been wounded, or Santiago pursuing his big fish? This deliberate blurring had always been in play, but now it seemed anxious, greedy. Or maybe not. Arch distrusted his growing aversion to both the man and the work. It might well be a dishonest form of chagrin at his own false position, or simply resentment at looking so small beside the giant to whom he'd let himself be linked.

But he was busy, and had greater cares than this. Helen. The various stages in his mother's long decline, and his sister's breakdown after her husband of thirty years discovered true love. A boy caught stealing. Papers to correct. A long miserable intrigue, never quite an affair, with the mother of a day boy from the village. Arch had little inclination to brood over this old foolishness about Hemingway, and indeed he hardly thought of it until some boy stared at him in a certain way, or stammered over a slight criticism of something in a Hemingway story as if afraid of offending him. Then he remembered. Such moments came and went, but never more than he could endure—not until the spring of 1961, when the headmaster announced that year's final visiting writer.

If Arch deserved punishment for this ludicrous myth of friendship, and he supposed he did, it began in earnest at that moment. He hadn't even known that Hemingway had been invited; he thought they were talking to John Steinbeck. They'd kept the news from him as a surprise, a *treat.* He soon learned that some anonymous alum had ponied up a small fortune to close the deal, but of course the boys assumed that Arch himself had swung it on pure goodwill. He could see them grinning at him even as the headmaster made the announcement. And it kept getting worse. That terrible, ubiquitous poster, all whiskers and teeth. The way the boys looked at him—their knowingness. And when they weren't impersonating Nick Adams they were pummelling their typewriters—it seemed that half the graduating class had a story in the works.

Arch was sick of these competitions. The headmaster had launched them years ago to encourage more boys to try their hand at writing, and at the time Arch had seen merit in the idea, but it soon palled on him. The scramble to win a private audience set them against one another and sanctioned the idea of writing as warfare by other means, with a handful of champions waving the bloody shirt over a mob of failed pretenders.

The other contests had been bad enough, but this one took on a frenzied, even delirious tone. So many boys tried to get Arch to read their stories that he posted a notice on his office door explaining that any help he gave would disqualify a manuscript from consideration. So it came as a relief when Hemingway chose a story—Arch had wondered if the great man would really go to the trouble—and brought the thing to an end.

The story itself surprised him. He'd read a few other pieces by the boy who wrote it, one of that ponderous *Troubadour* crowd, and found them predictably competent and labored. Standard schoolboy fare. Ramsey had told him this one was different, and it was. More Fitzgerald in it than Hemingway. Arch read it at breakfast the day it came out and again that night. He admired its art but was most affected, and in fact discomfited, by its unblinking inventory of self-seeking and duplicity. It was hard to tell the truth like that.

Arch was scolding a sixth former for cutting classes when the headmaster came to his office door and asked for a word. He looked tired. Arch sent the boy away and dismissed the evildoers waiting in the hall. He closed the office door and took the envelope the headmaster held out to him. The headmaster sat in one of the chairs facing the desk, and Arch was aware of his gaze as he went to his own chair and opened the envelope. It contained a page from an old number of the literary review of Miss Cobb's Academy.

Arch read the page and slipped it back into the envelope. I can't throw him out, he said.

Of course you can throw him out. We *have* to throw him out.

You can. I can't.

Arch, come on. You bounced Tompkins fast enough for swiping those shirts—pretty small beer compared to stealing someone's story.

I understand, Arch said.

Not to mention bamboozling Ernest Hemingway. For Pete's sake, we throw them out for cutting *chapel*. I had hopes for this boy, but we can't start playing favorites. You have what you need right there. The headmaster put his hands on his knees and leaned forward as if to push himself up.

I have to resign, Arch said.

The hell you say! Do your job.

From the school, Arch said. He hadn't known he would say this, but there it was.

What is this? Does the boy have something on you?

No.

Well?

Arch began to explain. He wasn't used to talking about himself, and did it clumsily, but he tried to make the headmaster understand. This boy had laid false claim to a story, whereas he himself had laid false claim to much more—to a kind of importance, to a life not his own. He had been in violation of the Honor Code for many years now and had no right to punish lesser offenders, especially this one, who'd been caught up in a hysteria for which Arch held himself partly responsible.

I'm kicking myself out, he said. That's my last act as dean.

The headmaster had listened closely to all of this. He said, So you don't know Hemingway.

Never laid eyes on the man.

Well, I for one never heard you say you did. Have you?

No. But I had a good idea what people thought.

You never once mentioned Hemingway in a personal connection?

Arch saw the emerging outline of an argument by which he could squirm off the hook, and he was touched and saddened that for his sake the headmaster would involve himself in cunning stratagems.

Thank you, John, he said. Bless your heart. I really do have to go.

Arch went to live with his older sister Margaret in Syracuse. They were close, he and Margaret, and had been since childhood when their father, a doctor, died of TB and their mother fell into the hands of one Madame von Ranke and her son Hermann. The von Rankes were spiritualists. They conducted grief-shocked Miriam to the very portals of the Higher Realm, where her departed husband issued pledges of abiding love and some very pointed business tips. Arch could still smell the licorice scent of Hermann's pomade; he could close his eyes anywhere and smell it. They robbed Miriam blind, until finally she had to sell the Ward Wellington Ward house on Euclid Avenue and move in with her old parents, children in tow. In their mother's cause Arch and Margaret became friends, but Margaret was a whiner and a crab and nowadays Arch couldn't last more than a couple of weeks at a time with her.

So he took trips. He passed part of the fall at Saranac Lake, not far from the sanitorium where his father had died. He drove up to Toronto and Montreal and down to New York, and that winter he spent some time with a Cornell classmate in Phoenix. The day after he arrived Arch visited the columbarium where Helen's ashes were buried. *Columbarium* was the word the funeral home had used in its letter, but it was no more than a small cinderblock courtyard in a windblown cemetery where the city gave out into hardpan and scrub.

Arch found the granite plaque with Helen's name on it and laid some flowers across it and stood there a while. They had met when he rented horses at the stable she ran in Brooklyn. She started riding with him, and invited him along on a few jaunts with the Lower Hudson Hunt Club. Arch had taken up riding only after his leg got bunged up, but he cut a fine figure on a horse and drove at a fence as hard as she did, and maybe this had misled her, because off a horse he was not the same man. On the ground he could neither lead nor follow her.

He wandered the cemetery, reading inscriptions. On his way back to the parking lot he saw a coyote trot across the grounds, and felt better about leaving Helen there.

He lived with Margaret, took his trips, and checked the mail for an expression of interest from one of the many schools he'd written to. He didn't really expect any result. As dean he had vetted such inquiries himself and shaken his head at their implausibility. Why would a man with thirty years and a position of respect in a good school suddenly throw it over to start again? He was too old. It didn't make sense. You just knew there was a story behind it, and one best not repeated in your own school.

Arch knew all the arguments against him, but he'd sent the letters anyway. He regretted quitting his job. He had regretted it that very morning, but didn't know how to undo what he'd done. Up to the moment he resigned he must have imagined that teaching was a distraction from some greater destiny still his for the taking. Of course he hadn't said this to himself, but he'd surely felt it, he later decided, because how else could he not have known how useless he would be thereafter? For thirty years he had lived in conversation with boys, answerable to their own sense of how things worked, to their skepticism, and, most gravely, to their trust. Even when alone he had read and thought in their imagined presence, made responsible by it, enlivened and honed by it. Now he read in solitude and thought in solitude and hardly felt himself to be alive.

But toward the end of winter Arch was invited to discuss an opening at St. John's Military Academy in Manlius, just a few miles up the road from Syracuse. He knew this had been arranged at the urging of Cal Meigs, a former student who now taught at St. John's, because Cal had called a few days before the official letter arrived to ask if Arch was still looking. Cal said that he'd become an English teacher because of Arch and couldn't imagine anything better than being on the same faculty with him.

I'm sure you had a good reason for leaving the sacred grove, Cal said.

I thought so, Arch said.

He drove to Manlius on a day of rare brilliant light and found Cal waiting at the gate, stamping his feet against the cold. Arch had no clear memory of him as a boy and certainly did not recognize this hollow-cheeked, mournful-looking man with the droopy red moustache, though he pretended to. Cal led him up a path between stone buildings barricaded by high walls of snow. Icicles glittered along the eaves. He slowed his pace for Arch and pointed things out, but Arch was watching the boys walk past him on their way to class. They wore handsome military great-coats and caps with gleaming bills, and their breath came out in white puffs as they talked and laughed.

The interview didn't last long. After a few questions about Arch's availability and what courses he might teach, the department chairman asked him why he'd left his old school.

That's a private matter, Arch said. He saw Cal look down at the table and was sorry to have put him in this spot.

We're going to need something more than that, the chairman said. He gazed around the table at his four colleagues, all of them looking anywhere but at Arch. Frankly, Mr. Makepeace, some of us have questions about your application. *I* have questions.

Certainly, Arch said, but it was a private decision and it will remain private.

The chairman looked around the table. That's it for me, he said. Any other questions? There were no other questions. Then he pushed his chair back and everyone stood. He shook hands with Arch. I understand you were a friend of Ernest Hemingway. My condolences, sir. And thank you for coming out today, he said. Thank you for your interest in St. John's.

Margaret had been sure Arch would get the job, and did not hide her bitter suspicion that he had spoiled the interview deliberately. I thought you wanted to teach, she said.

Yes, he wanted to teach, but that wasn't all Arch wanted, as he'd understood when the boys he'd seen that morning gazed past him without a flicker of interest. What more could he expect? Nothing, of course, yet his disappointment told him that he *had* expected more, being among schoolboys again, as if they would recognize him just because they were schoolboys. But if they saw anything at all it was just a standard-issue old fart tapping along the path, watching out for ice.

In former times Arch had supposed that his sense of being a distinctive and valuable man proceeded from his own qualities, and that they would sustain him in that confidence wherever he happened to be. He'd never imagined that this surety was conferred on him by others, by their knowing and cherishing him. But so it was. Unrecognized, he had become a ghost, even to himself.

He distilled no general rule from this understanding. Maybe a man of lordly self-conviction and detachment could forsake the place that knew him and not become a ghost. Arch could say only that he was not that man. He was attached. How could he have thought that he was free to leave his school?

At breakfast the boys were dull and bleary, and he missed the pleasure of needling them with his own morning crispness and cheer, asking bright questions, urging prunes on picky fellows who could barely stomach a piece of dry toast. The dorms gave forth a singular din at night—fifty different records playing at once, doors slamming, loud voices in long hallways, the faint hiss of many showers all running together. Arch always stopped to listen when he crossed the quad, as another man might linger on the call of a distant owl. He missed the tumult in the hallways between classes, and how the boys parted to make a path for him. He missed their noise and their woolly smell and their deep silence in chapel. He missed their good manners. He missed bucking them up when they got homesick or discouraged, and surprising them with his forbearance when they ran aground— hadn't they figured him out yet, after all these years? He missed how the boys went crazy in the first snowfall, and broke into song at any excuse, and forgot themselves in the excitement of finding something interesting in a poem, especially if Arch hadn't seen it. He missed all of that, and knowing the people around him, and being known. He missed a certain shy glance in which he saw respect and warmth and even some wonder. Arch wanted that back, as much as the rest. He wanted it all back.

In his next letter to his friend Ramsey, he said that he'd made a terrible mistake in leaving and would come back if given the chance. Ramsey would understand that this message was intended for the headmaster, to whom Arch could not write directly for fear of official rejection and the loss of all hope of return. Neither could he play the beggar after the noble pose he'd struck during their last meeting, when he'd brushed aside the headmaster's attempts to rethink the problem as if his old friend were trying to steal his soul, like some phantasm of moral paranoia in a Hawthorne story.

And as for that, had he learned nothing from all those years of teaching Hawthorne? Through story after story he'd led his boys to consider the folly of obsession with purity—its roots sunk deep in pride, flowering in condemnation and violence against others and oneself. For years Arch had traced this vision of the evil done through intolerance of the flawed and ambiguous, but he had not taken the lesson to heart. He had given up the good in his life because a fault ran through it. He was no better than Aylmer, murdering his beautiful wife to rid her of a birthmark.

Ramsey wrote back to say the headmaster would not respond unless he heard from Arch himself, and that it was impossible to know just what his thoughts were. He'd given nothing away. Write to him, please, Ramsey said. What can you lose?

Before he could stop himself Arch took a sheet of stationery from the drawer and drafted his plea. He apologized to the headmaster for deserting his post and asked to be taken back on whatever terms were possible. He knew that a man had been hired to replace him, so he did not expect to resume his former schedule of classes or to reoccupy his old digs. He would be happy to teach remedial classes and do some tutoring. As for lodgings, he could take a room in the village. He would certainly understand if nothing could be found for him, and sent his best wishes to everyone.

The headmaster replied by registered mail. He'd hoped Arch would decide to come back, he said, and for that reason had carried him as absent-on-leave. The new man had been hired for the year only. Arch would teach his usual classes and the apartment would be available on his return.

He did have two provisions for Arch to consider. The first was that he would no longer serve as dean. The second, that he would let sleeping dogs lie where Hemingway was concerned and make no attempt to set the record straight. At this late date it would only confuse the boys, to no purpose. If Arch was in accord, the headmaster, along with the masters and boys of the school, looked forward with enthusiasm to his return. He'd sent two copies of the letter. In earnest of his agreement, Arch was to sign and mail back the original in the enclosed envelope. The other he should keep for his own records.

Arch wouldn't have expected to go back as dean, or to use the boys as his confessors, but that there should be conditions of any kind, and stipulated in so cool a tone, made him know how far he had fallen in his friend's regard. The headmaster could not feign warmth when he didn't feel it, and Arch had watched other men writhe under that stony gaze for months and even years. Now it would be his turn. This was the only condition he hesitated to accept, but he accepted it.

Margaret gave him the silent treatment for a while when she heard the news, then relented and coddled him like a child about to leave home for the first time. They drove over to Saratoga for a weekend at the races and won almost three hundred dollars, which they parlayed into a series of long, sodden dinners at the only French restaurant in town. One night Margaret let it drop that Hermann von Ranke had been their mother's lover. Arch stared down at his plate.

You really didn't know? Margaret said. Well, what did you think? Lonely, foolish woman. Stupid. She was, Arch, she was! Stupid, stupid, stupid! Margaret burst into tears, and he had to take her hand and soothe her while the people around them tried to carry on as if nothing had happened.

In early August Arch got a letter from the headmaster's secretary saying that his apartment was ready. He'd had enough of Margaret and Syracuse, but the thought of returning to the school made him skittish. He put it off until the last possible day, when the faculty was due to assemble for their traditional preterm conference at the headmaster's house. Though he'd given himself enough time for the drive, he took a wrong turn outside Worcester on a route he'd travelled for years, then got lost again while backtracking and arrived at the school nearly an hour late. No time for a change of clothes, let alone a shower and shave. He fished a tie from one of the boxes on the backseat, but his fingers were stiff and he kept flubbing the knot. Finally he stopped and looked down the tunnel of leafy trees overhanging the lane. He did not drive away. He adjusted the rearview mirror and coaxed his tie into a perfect knot, then eased himself out of the car. Standing up after all these hours of driving made him lightheaded, and he steadied himself against the roof of the car. It was late afternoon, the air heavy and fragrant with the smell of cut grass. He took his stick out of the back and started up the lane.

Arch heard them well before he got to the house. They were in the headmaster's garden. Of course—they always gathered for drinks there before getting down to business. It sounded as if they'd been drinking, their voices loud, hilarious. A blue haze of smoke hung over the garden. As he came in under the rose-covered trellis someone yelled Arch! *Ecce homo!* and every head turned.

Arch stopped and looked down the garden to where the headmaster stood by the drinks table with another master. The headmaster said, Late for his own funeral! and everyone laughed, then he put his glass down and came toward Arch with both hands outstretched. Though the headmaster was the younger man, and much shorter, and though Arch was lame and had white hairs coming out of his ears and white stubble all over his face, he felt no more than a boy again—but a very well-versed boy who couldn't help thinking of the scene described by these old words, surely the most beautiful words ever written or said: His father, when he saw him coming, ran to meet him.

A Note on the Type

The text of this book has been set in Goudy Old Style, one of the more than one hundred typefaces designed by Frederic William Goudy (1865–1947). Although Goudy began his career as a bookkeeper, he was so inspired by the appearance of several newly published books from the Kelmscott Press that he devoted the remainder of his life to typography in an attempt to bring a better understanding of the movement led by William Morris to the printers of the United States.

Produced in 1914, Goudy Old Style reflects the absorption of a generation of designers with things "ancient." Its smooth, even color combined with its generous curves and ample cut marks it as one of Goudy's finest achievements.

Composed by Creative Graphics, Inc.,
Allentown, Pennsylvania

Printed and bound by R.R.Donnelley & Sons,
Harrisonburg, Virginia

Designed by Johanna S. Roebas